Brian O'Nolan wrote under the pen names of Flann O'Brien and Myles na Gopaleen. He was born in 1911 in Co. Tyrone. A resident of Dublin, he graduated from University College after a brilliant career as a student (editing a magazine called *Blather*), and joined the Civil Service, in which he eventually attained a senior position. He died in Dublin on 1 April 1966. His novels include *At Swim-Two-Birds*, *The Dalkey Archive*, *The Third Policeman*, *The Hard Life* and *The Poor Mouth* (originally published in Irish as *An Béal Bocht*).

D1464701

By the same author

The Third Policeman
At Swim-Two-Birds
The Hard Life
The Poor Mouth
The Dalkey Archive
Stories and Plays
The Hair of the Dogma
Further Cuttings from Cruiskeen Lawn
Myles Away from Dublin
The Best of Myles
Myles Before Myles

FLANN O'BRIEN
(Myles na Gopaleen)

The Various Lives of Keats and Chapman

and

The Brother

Edited and introduced by Benedict Kiely

PALADIN
GRAFTON BOOKS

A Division of the Collins Publishing Group

LONDON GLASGOW
TORONTO SYDNEY AUCKLAND

Paladin
Grafton Books
A Division of the Collins Publishing Group
8 Grafton Street, London W1X 3LA

Published in Paladin Books 1990

First published in Great Britain by
Hart-Davis, MacGibbon Ltd 1976

Copyright © 1976 by Evelyn O'Nolan
Introduction © 1976 by Benedict Kiely

ISBN 0-586-08952-7

Printed and bound in Great Britain by
Collins, Glasgow

Set in Plantin

All rights reserved. No part of this publication
may be reproduced, stored in a retrieval system,
or transmitted, in any form, or by any means,
electronic, mechanical, photocopying, recording or
otherwise, without the prior permission of
the publishers.

This book is sold subject to the condition that
it shall not, by way of trade or otherwise, be
lent, re-sold, hired out or otherwise circulated
without the publisher's prior consent in any
form of binding or cover other than that
in which it is published and without a similar
condition including this condition being
imposed on the subsequent purchaser.

Contents

Acknowledgements   viii

Preface   ix

The Various Lives of Keats and Chapman

Introduction: The Game of Keats and Chapman   3
1   The Right Sort of Frog   15
2   The Odd Guinea   16
3   Sherry and Bézique   18
4   Carnival   19
5   A Thing of Duty   20
6   Sun-struck Pigeons   21
7   Down the High   23
8   On Vesuvius   24
9   A Guinness   25
10   Wehrmacht   26
11   Zurich Tramcars   27
12   Up a Tree   28
13   The Manchester School   29
14   Hatter's Castle   30
15   Cats and Dustbins   31
16   In the Coffin   32
17   On Tour in France   33
18   Stradivarius   34
19   Arran Banners   35
20   African King   36
21   The Boots of Cortez   37
22   Coffee for One   38
23   Meeting of the Waters   39
24   Swans on Dog-leads   40
25   On the Tram   41
26   Boiling Porridge   42
27   Some Dread Disease   43
28   A Monkish Garment   44
29   Empty Heaven   45
30   Wild Sheep   46
31   Warts   47
32   The Delights of Bray   48
33   And Heidelberg   49
34   The Battle of Ventry   50

35	Rare China	51
36	Festina Lente	53
37	At Charing Cross	54
38	A Greek Colony	55
39	Wedding Presents	56
40	In the Highlands	58
41	The Coiner	59
42	A Man Called Dunne	60
43	Chapman's Bears	61
44	A Bite of Supper	62
45	Dentistry	63
46	Lions	64
47	Bombay Harbour	65
48	Hats and Leggings	66
49	Steel	67
50	Chapman's Castle	68
51	Man of Music	70
52	The X-Ray Eye	72
53	From Readers	73
54	Drunken Driving	75
55	A Millionaire	76
56	Gardeners	77
57	Chapman in Love	78
58	Espionage	79
59	Mineral Wealth	81
60	Burning Calf	82
61	Eugenics and Horseplay	83
62	Runaway Gelding	84
63	Storm in a Teacup	85
64	Walden Pond	87
65	Not Cricket	89
66	Beside the Brook	90
67	Paris Fashions	91
68	Mexican Dog	92
69	Triple Murder	93
70	Haute Cuisine	95
71	A National Note	96
72	Warp and Woof	98
73	Do It Yourself	99
74	The Fire of Genius	100
75	Witch-doctor's Brew	101
76	On an Urn	102
77	From the Vasty Deep	103
78	To Be Beside the Sea	104
79	Party of Poets	105

80 The Powder of Life   106
81 A One-Man Keats   107
82 The Iron Horse   108
83 The Road to Nowhere   109
84 Watt's That?   110
85 Turner and Lane   111

The Brother

Introduction: Utrum Frater Sit?   115
Part One   119
Part Two   140
Books by Flann O'Brien   157

Acknowledgements

The 'Keats and Chapman' stories in this volume originally appeared in the *Cruiskeen Lawn* column which Flann O'Brien wrote for *The Irish Times* under the pseudonym Myles na Gopaleen. The publishers would like to thank the editor and proprietors of the *Irish Times* for their kind permission in allowing us to reproduce this work.

'The Brother' is the edited text of Eamon Morrissey's stage adaptation based on 'The Brother' character who originally appeared in the *Cruiskeen Lawn* column of *The Irish Times*. It also includes material which originally appeared in Flann O'Brien's various published novels. The publishers would again like to thank the editor and proprietors of *The Irish Times* for permission to reproduce and adapt this work. We would also like to thank Mrs Evelyn O'Nolan, the author's widow, and Eamon Morrissey for allowing the work to be reproduced in this volume.

Preface

When I was at University College, Dublin, there were three men called Kevin O'Nolan in more or less the same year. Their names took variant forms, ranging from Caoimhghin O Nuallain by way of Kevin Nolan to Kevin B. Nowlan. One of the three, I'm sorry to say, I've lost trace of; the other two are still to be found in UCD, one of them a professor of history, the other a professor of classics, and one of them is the brother of Myles na Gopaleen or Flann O'Brien or Brian O Nuallain (Brian O'Nolan). I mention this matter because the idea or symbol of trinity seems to go with the name of Flann O'Brien as the idea of 'twinity' is dealt with in such detail in John Barth's *The Sotweed Factor*.

In 1968, one of the three Kevins, the brother of Brian, edited and prefaced, under the title *The Best of Myles*, a selection from the humorous, satirical, learned, grave-faced, crazy writing that his triply named brother put into a newspaper column in the Dublin daily *The Irish Times* from 1939 until his death in 1966.

Learned professors and their ways did now and again get the hard knock in that column, which was called 'Cruiskeen Lawn' or 'The Full Little Jug' after a famous old drinking song that begins: 'Let the farmer praise his grounds, let the huntsman praise his hounds.' But the praise of the singer is reserved for a jugful of the best: a sentiment with which the columnist, no different from many of us, had no quarrel.

Now it happened that in UCD in those distant days there was a nervous professor of economics who feared that some day he might be pilloried in the column as some of his colleagues had been – with the result that he always went out of his way to be pleasant to one of the three Kevins, thinking him to be the brother of the columnist. The fact that it was the wrong Kevin did not subtract a laugh from the humour of the situation.

It all did go to show the remarkable influence that that most peculiar newspaper column had. Myles was feared, as were some of the ancient Gaelic poets who it was said could deprive, disfigure, or even kill, with a satire. There was no malice in him but he could set the town laughing, and a pity for you if the laughter were at your expense.

The column began in Irish, came finally to be written almost entirely in English, and had its moments even in an odd pidgin that was *eadar eatorra* or betwixt and between, nor did the author on occasion despise French or the classical languages. There had been nothing like it since that strange Cork priest who didn't practise, Francis Sylvester Mahony, friend of Thackeray, invented the character of Father Prout, the parish priest of Watergrasshill, Co. Cork, and wrote for *Fraser's Magazine* 'The Rogueries of Tom Moore'.

The pseudonym that Myles used came from a character in Gerald Griffin's nineteenth-century novel *The Collegians* – the nickname of a roving Kerry horse-trader, Myles of the Little Horses. Once when I so translated it, Myles devoted a full column to arguing against my translation, and with a weight of classical reference defended, as against the horse, big or little, the autonomy of the pony. Griffin's novel *The Collegians* had also two other lives, one as a play *The Colleen Bawn* by Dion Boucicault, the other as an opera *The Lily of Killarney*.

The column is at present being spasmodically rerun in *The Irish Times* and it is likely that as long as that newspaper exists the best of Myles will continue to be part of it. This is only as it should be. Few newspapers ever had such a column, as the aforementioned volume,[1] edited by Kevin O'Nolan, will readily show. For Myles could extract wisdom and fun and wicked mockery out of the oddest, most unlikely subjects, even out of technical talk about the driving of railway engines; nor have I ever met anyone who could tell me whence he derived his copious and, I have been told, exact information. The more rigid, old-fashioned Gaelic revivalists were driven up the wall by his mockery – in Irish and in that rare mixture of Irish and English – of their idiosyncrasies. Yet the very style of this mockery was one good proof that a revival had, in

---

[1] *The Best of Myles*, a selection from 'Cruiskeen Lawn' by Myles na Gopaleen (Flann O'Brien), edited and with a preface by Kevin O'Nolan (Hart-Davis, MacGibbon: London, 1968).

fact, taken place. He had a sore way with false pretenders to culture and invented for their benefit experts to 'handle' their books, so that their books would appear to have been read; and ventriloquists for hire who, in the theatre and other public places, would carry on, in the voices of their patrons, very audible and cultured conversations.

He had a delicate ear for the ordinary talk of the Dublin streets and pubs, and in the column made great play with the truth that behind every decent, average, genuine, native Dublinman there is another man who is not just a brother but 'the Brother'. He had an ingenious way with imaginary gadgets and some of the inventions – particularly the snow gauge – of the imaginary Myles na Gopaleen Research Bureau merit their place among the best in the world of know-how. He had a wide fantasy world ranging from these exploits of Keats and Chapman to the dynasty of Sir Myles na Gopaleen the da and Sleeveen na Gopaleen, his daughter.

Above all he was a well-read scholarly man and mad about words. As he put it himself: 'I am, of course, intensely interested in education. I have every reason to be because I was disabled for life at the age of fifteen by a zealous master (although I had the laugh on him afterwards when I came back from hospital with my two hands amputated).'

That was an odd dark sort of humour that he was to develop to eternity in *The Third Policeman*.

To come back to the trinity or the rule of three or what-you-will.

He himself was, as I've said, three men. Under the name he got, or took, by birth and at the baptismal font, he was Brian O'Nolan, an Irish senior civil servant with a knowledge of administration, and what went on behind it, that could prove disconcerting to his colleagues when he dissected them under his name of Myles na Gopaleen. As Myles, also, he was the author of that satire in Irish *An Béal Bocht* (*The Poor Mouth*) in which, at one and the same time and even more than in his Irish–English cavortings in his column, he satirized the Gaelic revival and proved that the revival had succeeded in so far as such a book could be written at all. As Flann O'Brien he wrote *At Swim-Two-Birds*, a novel within a novel within a novel within a novel, and so on. At the beginning of which he stoutly maintained: 'One beginning and one ending for a book is a thing I did not agree with. A good book may have three openings entirely dissimilar and inter-related only in the prescience of the author.' Under the same name he wrote *Faustus Kelly*, a play for the Abbey Theatre, and an Irish version of Capek's *Insect Play*, three other novels, *The Hard Life*, *The Dalkey Archive*, and *The Third Policeman*, and some lesser writings. The macabre humour of *The Third Policeman* came to light and to life twenty-seven years after it was written and a year or so after the author's death: and, oddly enough, it is a most sardonic novel of life after death with a dead man telling the comic and terrifying tale.

The life-story of *At Swim-Two-Birds* was quite as extraordinary as the life-story, or death-story, of *The Third Policeman*. First published in London just before the war, it won the admiration of James Joyce, Graham Greene, William Saroyan, and practically nobody else except an in-group at UCD who took to talking in its phrases. A large part of the first edition was blitzed (unknowingly) by the Germans. Republished after the war it began to attract the critical attention it deserved as an uncanny playing about with the mechanics of the novel. Graham Greene, not unnaturally concerned with those mechanics, had talked of the pleasure you feel when you see somebody smashing glass on the stage. Anthony Burgess said excellently: 'What a fuss the French anti-novelists make about their tedious experiments in *chosisme*; how little fuss has been made about Flann O'Brien's humour, humanity, metaphysics, theology, bawdrey, mythopoeia, word-play and six-part counterpoint.'

O'Brien can set one laughing, marvelling at his odd learning, his wealth of words, and at the same time he can set one wondering, in an instructive and profitable way, about the whole shape and make of the novel, even about its many, or any, reasons for existing. John Barth's Ebenezer Cooke in *The Sotweed Factor* found it impossible to pick on any one calling in life because all callings were so entrancing. Flann O'Brien plays whack with the novel – not because it is impossible to tell a story any more but because he is mobbed by stories and characters and situations. His playful suggestion that novels should be made up of stock characters taken out of all previous novels is not as playful as it might seem. He could, and did, use with great effect passages from a musty old *Conspectus of the Arts and Sciences*, and from a long-forgotten poem, by one Falkiner, about a shipwreck and such enlivening matters as the taking of the azimuth; and could set a character talking wittily about the proper way to read a gas meter.

Even the bare outline of *At Swim-Two-Birds* gives some idea of his bizarre method. A student in University College, Dublin, indulges in 'spare-time literary activities' which take the form of writing a book about Dermot Trellis,[2] an eccentric author who 'conceives the project of writing a salutary book on the consequences which follow wrong-doing'. For his purpose Trellis creates these characters: the Pooka Fergus Mac Phellimey, 'a species of human Irish devil endowed with magical powers'; John Furriskey, 'a depraved character whose task is to attack women and behave at all times in an indecent manner'; Peggy, a domestic servant, whom Trellis instructs Furriskey to betray but with whom Furriskey honourably falls in love – thereby displaying a Pirandelloish independence of character from author; and Fionn MacCool, 'a legendary character hired by Trellis on account of his venerable appearance to act as the girl's father and chastise her for transgressions against the moral law', but who actually assails Peggy's virtue.

In addition to these the novel, or what-you-will, finds

---

[2] About *At Swim-Two-Birds* J. C. C. Mays writes: 'The book that Brian O'Nolan's Stephen-figure is writing centres on the dreams of a publican, a "night-logic" world which obeys its own laws and appears to be liberated from customary physical restraints, all its characters merging into one another around a small core of fixed types. Even the choice of the name Trellis is not without significance when one recalls Joyce's remark to Padraic Colum, "Of course, I don't take Vico's speculations literally; I use his cycles as a trellis." The extent to which the use of Joyce controls the organisation of *At Swim-Two-Birds* is indicated by the fate of Brinsley. Whereas in fact, as Brian O'Nolan's good friend, Niall Sheridan, he is included in the plot as the friend and adviser he was, his role as a Cranly figure overtakes him: he is felt in some way, only explicable in terms of the parody, to have betrayed the narrator.' See *Myles: Portraits of Brian O'Nolan*, edited by Timothy O'Keeffe (Martin Brian and O'Keeffe: London, 1973).

room for Mad Sweeney, another legendary character, the account of whose madness and sufferings, and whose recitation of bardic staves, gloriously plays games with ancient legend and literature; for Casey, the working man's poet, author of the noble poem 'A Pint of Plain is Your Only Man'; for Tracy, the author of fantastic western thrillers, and some of the Dublin cowpokes who take part in his stories; for the Good Fairy who plays poker from the Pooka's pocket; for the biographical reminiscences of the university student, and for his sober uncle and his frequently boozed friends.

Summarizing is a thankless task and does little towards giving a picture of the uproarious world that revolved in this strange man's imagination. Yet, in passing, one may squeeze in a reference to Father Kurt Fahrt, SJ, a German Jesuit in the Irish province, and to Mr Collopy who became so heavy from drinking the gravid water concocted by his nephew who could walk (almost) on air that he met his death by falling through the stairs of La Scala in Milan. They and their learned discussions, and the secret project that Mr Collopy put before the Pope, are to be found in the novel *The Hard Life*.

The dedication to that novel reads: 'I honourably present to Graham Greene, whose own forms of gloom I admire, this misterpiece.' When I reviewed the novel for a Dublin newspaper, I had a letter, enclosing papal blessing, from Father Kurt Fahrt, SJ. The letter-writer could have been any one of three men.

The Third Policeman may already have more than challenged *At Swim-Two-Birds* for the title of pre-eminence among the four novels of Flann O'Brien.

In it, a young and rather strange countryman who is interested in an obscure philosopher called de Selby[3] takes part in

---

[3] In *At Swim-Two-Birds* Niall Sheridan, or the character based on him, is called Brinsley for, more or less, these reasons: he was (he still is) a Meath man, an Irish midlander, as was the novelist and Abbey Theatre playwright Brinsley MacNamara – Meath and Westmeath, about which Brinsley MacNamara wrote his most celebrated novel, *The Valley of the Squinting Windows*, being two halves of the one whole.

Brinsley MacNamara's real name was John Weldon but, originally for the stage and afterwards for his writing, he preferred a grander a crude, brutal, very Irish-rural murder and robbery. De Selby and his egregious commentators, Hatchjaw, Bassett, Kraus, du Garbandier, *et al.*, follow the narrative, 'bald heads forgetful of their sins', in a series of footnotes. This is, if you like, an academic game, the game of a bright young classical student who has just realized that Madvig and Zumpt, or at any rate the names of those eminent men, have comic possibilities. But it is brilliantly done, and de Selby's theories on the nature of darkness (black air) and on the illusion of movement may long be considered.

So much for the footnotes. On the open printed page when the young man goes to a dark house to collect the loot from the robbery he is, by the malice of his accomplice, blown to bits. Thereafter, he wanders in a strange place of pleasant but uncannily stilled landscapes where people are part bicycles and bicycles part people, where all one-legged men have united in one murderous army. In that place the proper way to build a gallows can be discussed in a friendly and academic fashion between builder-executioner and destined victim. There is also an underground realm called Eternity with

---

scansion. We Irish are great name-changers. Myles once wrote that Seán Ó Faoláin (to whom all honour) and myself had one thing in common: we wrote under our own names. He added: 'A dangerous thing to do.' The kernel of the joke was that Seán Ó Faoláin was using the Gaelic (Irish) version of his name.

Anyway: Niall Sheridan's favourite party piece was, and still is, an affectionate and startlingly real impersonation of Brinsley MacNamara telling a comic story. Brinsley is no longer with us but Sheridan's uncanny impersonation can, to those who loved him and laughed with him, still make him visible.

On a more scholarly level, Niall Sheridan was the first person to point out what *The Third Policeman* owes to Huysmans' *A Rebours*. J. C. C. Mays has elaborated on this (see op. cit., p. 92–5). The matter is gone into in careful detail, leading to these and other conclusions. 'The point is, though, that what for Huysmans was a world to be created and explored as a thing to be sought after is for Brian O'Nolan a thing of fascination but also of folly.'

And: 'The creation of a world which is demonstrably false, at which we can therefore laugh and yet from which we cannot escape, is the source of *The Third Policeman*'s strange magnetic attraction. It achieves Des Esseintes' ideal of hallucination through artifice, the substitution of 'le rêve de la réalité à la réalité même', but it does so to a different end. Brian O'Nolan's end is not anguish but fantasy, not the exotic and the perverse but the unbelievable proved, not neurosis but a world exhilarating and wrong.'

innumerable rooms all exactly alike – everything repeats and returns. It is grim fun, if it is fun.

The young man's two companions are two policemen: Sergeant Pluck, the Greatest Dead Authority on the Bicycle People and on the Law of the Interchange of Atoms (there is a shadow of him in Sergeant Fottrell in *The Dalkey Archive*, the fourth novel) and Policeman Mac Cruiskeen, who made a chest, or box, so beautiful that the only thing suitable to put into it was another, exactly similar, chest or box; and so on until the craftsman was working with invisible tools at chests and boxes no longer visible.

To find out who the third policeman is you must yourself make the journey to that undiscovered country. You may find it worth the trouble: keeping in mind that one part of the idea of *At Swim-Two-Birds* is the revolt of the creature against the creator; muttering for charms as you go the names of Joyce, Sterne, Gide, Huysmans, and Pirandello, even of that aforementioned Francis Sylvester Mahony who came to be known as Father Prout – but always returning to the name of Flann O'Brien, a strange, original, sombre, comic genius.

Since Flann O'Brien's (Brian O'Nolan's) late uncle, George Gormley, once sports editor of the Dublin *Evening Mail*, always argued, with a display of genealogical knowledge I can neither dispute nor verify, that he was second or third cousin to my uncle, Peter Gormley, I may be permitted some personal memories.

Once in the Ousel Galley in Dame Street – a bar whose odd history fascinated him and which, in a changing city, is no longer there – he delivered to a friend and myself a lecture on the importance of the chamber pot in Irish history. An enraptured audience gathered around. That day, too, we had a learned discussion about the Great Western Schism: not the one that you read about in the commonplace books of history but the one that happened when the Tory islanders refused to allow the departing Roman Catholic curate (whom they liked) off the island or the curate newly appointed by the bishop (whom they disliked) onto the island.

He had a still better story based on the known, or suspected, Norse nature of a people who regard Ireland as a foreign island and the plain people of Ireland as an untrustworthy people.

It seems that in the British days the islanders on one occasion resisted imperial administration and refused to pay the rates. So the British sent out of Galway a naval vessel, say a corvette, to see that the Tory people (nothing to do with Mrs Thatcher. See map) lived up to England's expectations and did their duty.

This, more or less in the words of the master as I recall them, is the end of the story: 'And can you tell me, Ben, what the Tory islanders did? They knelt down and prayed. God only knows who or what they prayed to, but pray they did. And furthermore. Can you tell me what happened to the British gunboat? It sank off Galway...(long pause)...with all hands on board.'

That consideration of whatever gods the sons of the Norse sea-rovers appealed to taking punitive action against the British navy delighted him. He told the story, as I said, in the bar then called the Ousel Galley – now lost in what they call development. The story of the original Ousel Galley, the ship, was another wellspring of delight. It was in the absurdity of things that sailors from Ringsend, the ancient port of Dublin, should be kidnapped by Barbary corsairs and robbed of their vessel and liberty, and that they should escape, steal back their vessel and everything else they could lay their hands on, and sail triumphantly home. Tracy's Dublin cowpokes, in *At Swim-Two-Birds*, who were very much at home in Ringsend, could have done no better.

The Various Lives of
Keats and Chapman

Introduction
Benedict Kiely

The Game of Keats and Chapman

It is a game. Not a book to be read straight.

A learned Jesuit, of whom even Flann O'Brien might have approved, told me that a man came to him once to ask him for a spiritual book to read. He gave him *The Imitation of Christ* by Thomas à Kempis. Next day the man was back. He had read that book and wanted another.

No more than à Kempis, the tales of Keats and Chapman are not to be treated with the haste which St Teresa of Avila said was the enemy of devotion. Take the tales one at a time and study the method. The fun then is in trying to do it yourself, in drawing out the tale, accumulating the fantasy to the point, as J. C. C. Mays has suggested, of sadism, then in crashing home with the flat desolating pun. For instance:

Peter O'Curry has a Keats and Chapman story which he once suggested to Myles but which he says never appeared in the column. Here are the bare bones of it, and to attempt to build flesh on them could prove an excellent exercise. Exotic elaboration carried out in the gravest possible manner is an essential part of the game. This is only a summary:

For various charges of drink and disorder Keats and Chapman are sentenced to Mountjoy jail; identical sentences. The behaviour of Keats while in prison is better than that of Chapman and his remissions, as a consequence, greater; so he is the first to be discharged. On his way out he calls to pay his respects to the governor. Who is not at home: and Keats, swept away by the romantic thing, makes over-ardent advances to the governor's wife and ends up back in his cell. On which Chapman says: 'Let that teach you not to end a sentence with a proposition.'

Or consider this one, also given here in summary. The full story in all its oily detail must be acknowledged to Seán Mac-Reamoinn.

Walking in poetic solitude on the seashore Keats has the good or ill fortune to encounter a mermaid with whom he falls in love. He captures her and deprives her of her cloak,

3

which is the way to retain the affections of a captured mermaid or, at any rate, to retain the mermaid. They live and love in a seaside villa, also inhabited by Chapman, who casts eyes, of a sort, on the mermaid. Famine strikes the land, the potatoes fail, or the EEC takes over. One day while Keats is away from home searching for food, Chapman burns the cloak and grills and eats the mermaid. When Keats returns Chapman tells him that by a subterfuge she has regained her cloak and fled back to her native sea. But an odour in the air and some bones in the trash-bin reveal the horrid truth, and the reproaches are bitter. Chapman's defence is to say: 'But, my dear fellow, one man's mate [meat] is another man's poisson.'

You get the idea and can elaborate on the stories as you please. Then think of your own fearful pun or think of your own story. Generally speaking, I'd say the pun would come before the story, but then that's a matter of accident, inspiration, individual style.

Neither of those two stories, as I've said, belonged to Myles, although they owed their original inspiration to him. Let him, then, tell in his own words how the whole crazy thing began. This statement appeared with comic illustrations by Warner, in the Dublin magazine *Social and Personal* for December 1951.

Let us accept that literature is a live, noble, pulsating thing – man's ever-growing testimony of his own unrepentant existence. I think it follows that this organism is as subject to disease as is man himself. Readers should therefore take rather seriously the illustrated tales about Keats and Chapman which begin with this issue of *Social and Personal*: for month by month will be unmasked a formidable corpus of studies in literary pathology. Things will get worse instead of better: ultimately the malady will spread from these pages to the most guarded reader – for this malady is infectious, contagious and pandemic.

Then Myles gives the dates of the birth and death of Keats, his vocation in life, a brief reference to his productivity even at his tender years – and quotes in full the celebrated sonnet 'On First Looking Into Chapman's Homer'. All of that we may here take as read. Myles proceeds:

In one respect Keats resembled the homely man who, venturing

4

abroad, is uncertain whether a dish he finds before him in a restaurant is simply last night's choked ash tray or the first course of a *recherché* meal: he was fascinated by Greek literature and mythology but knew no Greek.

And that is where Chapman came in. With other big fellows such as Pope, Hobbes and Ogilvy, Chapman rendered the works of Homer into English. Pope, decrying his predecessor, has complained that Chapman (Book 13, VR. 312, Odyssey) made twenty English verses out of two Greek. No matter, Chapman pleased Keats.

This is how the two men came together. About twelve years ago I wrote and published in *The Irish Times* – for no reason I can lucidly explain – the following little story:

'One day Chapman called to Keats's lodging, carrying a trained but disabled pigeon. The bird was very valuable and had a distinguished record in respect of secret communication duties in the late war. But it was very ill, having swallowed some foreign body which was lodged in the windpipe.

'Keats carefully put the fowl on his desk, fixed its claws down with adhesive tape and then, putting its beak agape with small wedges, peered down the passage with the aid of a dentist's tiny flash-lamp. A fragment of champagne cork was revealed and quickly extracted.

'Immediately, thereafter, the poet sat down (essential literary preliminary even for those already seated) and wrote a sonnet entitled "On First Looking into Chapman's Homer".'

The details of the examination and operation display the sort of corroborative detail that goes into the building up of a good episode in the various lives of Keats and Chapman. That phrase, by the way, I borrow from Brinsley MacNamara's novel *The Various Lives of Marcus Igoe*, in which a man in the Irish midlands lives in his mind many lives. The late and great (in many ways) R. M. Smyllie said that that was the novel that Brinsley had written backways, and on the flyleaf was the inscription from Montaigne: 'We are never present with but always beside ourselves.'

R. M. Smyllie, moustached and of huge girth, was the editor of *The Irish Times* who, against all wisdom inherited and gained from experience and against all the rules of all the books, engaged Brian O'Nolan to write a regular column. The marvellous combination worked like a charm.

One day years ago, in D'Olier Street, Dublin, at the back of *The Irish Times*, I saw an extraordinary sight. A large, stout man with a moustache stood, stolid as a statue, and puffed at a pipe and looked impassively in the general direction of Wexford – south and sixty miles away. Facing him a smaller man, with sharp active features, a dark overcoat swinging open, a wide-brimmed hat, talked like a controlled and directed tempest, and jabbed with a forefinger in the general direction of the stout man. The smoke of the pipe rose like incense above them. Or like the smoke from a railway engine.

Knowing what went on, one could guess that the vehement talk could have been about (a) more money for the column (b) some of the menacing letters and threats of legal action that the column could provoke (c) the advisability of removing some passage that might give rise to more menaces. That vision of editor and columnist will stay forever in my mind.

The story was told of Smyllie that once in an hotel in Liverpool, a short-sighted professor from Cork approached a table in the dining room to shake hands, as he thought, with R.M.S., to find himself instead intruding on the meditations of Mr Oliver Hardy. Smyllie never did think much of that joke.

All these details seem to me to have a relevance to the zany world of Myles na Gopaleen.

The first telling of the tale of the pigeon did not mean that the unfortunate bird was then dismissed in peace to his cote. Here follows another version:

When Keats was a boy he wanted to be a vet. His devotion to animals was shown by the interest he took in the pigeons which flocked around his house. In company with Chapman, the boy next door, he made pets of many of them and trained them to do all sorts of tricks – even to recite odd lines of poetry in a thick foreign accent. The science of training pigeons for military and courier duties was then in its infancy, but Keats and Chapman were unremitting in their efforts and succeeded in producing several first-rate homing birds. One day Chapman's favourite homing pigeon fell sick and the distressed owner looked to the veterinary-minded Keats for advice. Keats suspected croup. He placed the pigeon on a perch, forced open its beak with a tiny dentist's jaw-plug and peered down its throat with the aid of a flash-lamp. It is not recorded whether his diagnosis was correct or whether he effected a cure, but shortly afterwards he sat down and wrote the famous sonnet entitled 'On First Looking Into Chapman's Homer'.

And here is the most elaborate version of all, entitled 'The Small Fowl at Aalst'.

In addition to his standing as a poet, John Keats was highly qualified as agronomist, ornithologist, painter, political philosopher, sportsman and piano-tuner. The various tasks he was called upon to perform often entailed fatiguing travel, poor pay and provision for sustenance ranging from the modest to the very mean.

In the autumn of 1814 a monsigneur of the city of Aalst, Belgium, commissioned him to attend at the parish church there to rehang and put aright the bells of the carillon, which had been damaged during the excesses of the Napoleonic wars. When he arrived, he found he had been allotted lodgings in a particularly squalid quarter of the town. Staying temporarily here also while teaching English in the local lycée was a fellow Briton, Mr G. Chapman. He, by way of a hobby, indulged in the cultivation and study of carrier pigeons. He had a pigeon loft suspended at the eaves of the grim house but one evening Keats found that one pigeon, apparently ailing, was accommodated in a cage in the dining room.

The poet's interest was at once aroused. He brought the cage close to the large oil lamp on the table and closely studied the bird, using a pocket magnifying glass he never failed to carry. He suspected coccidiosis, gapes, croup, fowl cholera, and even the presence of dread *bacillus psitacosis*. But he could not be sure. He opened the cage, took out the bird, carefully fitted it into a tiny harness he usually had in his pocket. Having adjusted the bird on a cushion he broke a matchstick and used one portion to prop open its beak, tilting the head to the light to study the throat minutely with his glass. He was pleased to see that a particle of food was obstructing the gullet: this he shoved down with a small nail-file and restored the bird, now happy, to the cage.

Having pondered the operation, the poet then sat down and according to report wrote the sonnet headed 'On First Looking Into Chapman's Homer'.

When Chapman arrived later, the two men became firm friends.

It can be seen how, from a comparatively barren beginning, the legend has grown, gathering detail and an exotic background. From that moment onwards Keats and Chapman were to soldier on together in the oddest places and in many historical periods. They are to be found in Greyfriars where Billy Bunter went to school – or to the tuckshop; in the Vale of Avoca where Tom Moore sat under a tree and wrote a song; on the slopes of Vesuvius 'watching the bubbling lava and considering the sterile ebullience of the stony entrails of the earth', and making a dreadful pun about the drinking of whiskey. They are studying biochemistry in Munich, owning a pub in London, and being visited by Dr Watson from Baker Street. They are in Heidelberg 'arranging for the purchase of cheap doctorates', they are on a river estuary breeding swans for the sake of swansdown, or on a secret mission to India on behalf of the British Government, or on the music hall stage, or breeding a pedigree bull, or gambling in Ostend, or eating roes of tunny in an expensive restaurant and, once again, remembering Tom Moore: the world, indeed, is their oyster.

Nor must we forget that they are all the time in the middle of a newspaper column where all sorts of other things, and people, are going on around them. An ornithological treatise on the Russians and the common tern may lead into the story of why Keats wore a clawhammer coat (tails) when eating lobster. And why not? Or in the same column in which Keats is spilling milk in a cab (cabri-au-lait) Myles is threatening to write a book about a mythical Wild Goose: the Brigadier Remus O'Gorman of Cookstown. The Wild Geese were the Irish soldiers who went to fight in Continental armies at the end of the seventeenth century and after the Williamite wars but the name of Brigadier Remus may be an echo of the name of Brigadier Dorman Smith who gaelicized himself to Dorman O'Gowan.

Or in a column in which Chapman is training performing frogs for a circus (it's a wrong toad that has no learning), the Myles na Gopaleen Research Bureau is advertising the patent-spring-tophat for warding off falling chimney pots, bricks, slates, window sills, or iron balconies. This invention, we are told, is much needed in an old city like Dublin.

Less than a week after the publication of the tale of the ailing pigeon Myles tells us that the celebrated Jimmy Montgomery composed a story which Myles was to add to the canon in this fashion:

8

Keats's bubbling sense of humour is reflected in the following anecdote which the poet insisted on relating time out of number to the wretched Chapman, whose countenance had long since acquired the permanent look of suffering usually associated with music hall violinists.

'It is not generally known,' he would say, 'that Alexander the Great was allergic to eggs. He forbade the humble ovoid to all his men, and declared he would execute any person he found eating an egg or possessing one. Nevertheless, there was much secret egg-eating in his camp. One night, in making his rounds of the barracks, the king very nearly surprised a group of officers who were seated round the canteen fire *in flagrante delicto*. They were saved only by the presence of mind of a lance-corporal, who managed to warn his comrades and greet the king with the single inspired cry:

"All Eggs Under The Grate"!'[4]

Sometimes the stories don't rise, flattened by the repetition of a formula and the tyranny of the daily column. Often the story need have no connection, logical or otherwise, with the ensuing pun. Often the story may need the voice, the gesture, the glass of amber malt on the bar counter. It's a pub game rather than a parlour game: or a bar parlour game.

J. C. C. Mays, whom I quote copiously, for the good and sufficient reason that he has written the best critical study yet of Brien-Flann-Myles, says in the essay mentioned in the notes to this introduction that we laugh at a Keats and Chapman story for the reason Kant tells us that we should: 'from the sudden transfiguration of a strained expectation into nothing'. The pleasure derived from the stories may be, Mays says, 'the pleasure of anticipations belittled'. It is arguable that the 'meticulosity and the economy of their way of telling can only be called callous'. All that makes a deal of sense, and the critic relates it to other aspects of the three-headed writer.

[4] Jimmy Montgomery, one of the more celebrated Dublin wits, was father to Niall Montgomery, notable architect and Joyce commentator – and father also to more witty sayings than could even be attributed to him. There is a theory that other wits lived on his leavings. Like Myles he was fatally addicted to puns. When he was appointed, of all things, film censor, with the task of removing indecency and obscenity from the silver screens of Catholic Ireland, he said that his lot was most unenviable: he was between the devil and the Holy See.

Niall, his son, acted in secret at times as Myles and it could be a fine task of scholarly detection to identify his contributions.

Outside the lives of Keats and Chapman I pick at random from the column a fair sample of the callous. He has, he says, thought of something quite new in the way of stage plays:

My theory is that any play is bound to become tedious if it contains 'human' characters. We see far too much of these tiresome bipeds, and listening to them 'talking' (whether as themselves or some less absurd character devised by a playwright) is becoming an annoyance in this unamusing world. What I want to see is a theatre stage upon which is erected a shallow tank filled with mud and water. Enter Sir Séamus O'Shaughran, attired in the loud sporty tweeds of his class. Enter a poacher. Enter a gamekeeper. Next thing you hear is some *pizzicato* work on the violins, a clue that you have accidentally walked into a ballet orgy. The parties on the stage then embark on vast leppings and prancings, splashing about in the wet and churning up the muck. This goes on for hours until the needs of art have been satisfied.

Next day the play will inevitably be described as a flop. It is then and only then that we reveal that the players were sea-lions and seals and we urbanely enquire of the critics what those beasts are expected to achieve. What but a resounding watery flop.

He was writing that in the late 1940s and may, indeed, have been ahead of his time.

There are a few Keats and Chapman stories that I remember but I have been unable to find the texts. Here are summaries of my memories of three of them. On a day of brilliant sunshine Keats and Chapman are walking out in the country alongside a high hedgerow. From the field beyond the hedge they hear the measured tones of a verse-speaker. Verse-speakers and verse-speaking societies came in for quite a lot of badinage from Myles. The verse-speaker in the field is not, however, speaking verse. He is saying slowly: 'Two and two are four, two and three are five.' And so on. Keats says: ''Tis the bright day that bringeth forth the adder.'

Then, on another occasion, Keats comes home one evening to find Chapman seated under the table drinking some nauseous-smelling fluid out of a large vessel. On careful enquiry Keats finds out that Chapman has had a violent argument with a stranger in a pub, has enticed the man to the dwelling, stunned him with a blow, then dissolved him in acid. John George Haigh of the ageing ladies and the acid baths, who was very popular at the time, may have had some influence on that story. Chapman explains his eccentric behaviour to Keats: 'He dared me to drink him under the table.'

Chapman could only with difficulty have survived that adventure, yet he turns up again with Keats in a pub in Gardiner Street in the north of Dublin city. As bards of passion and of mirth Keats and Chapman are often found in taverns. In this particular tavern they get talking with a most argumentative man. He lives in the village of Swords, North County Dublin, and to Swords they go, where the argument continues in another pub. By this time Chapman is heartily sick of their new acquaintance. The argument is, as far as I remember, about art; and the Swordsman[5] says that he has in his house across the street a painting that would prove his point. So Keats and himself set out, somewhat intoxicated, to cross the street. Keats has the ill luck, while his companion adroitly leaps to safety, to be knocked down by a lorry and severely injured. Going to see him in hospital Chapman gloomily says: 'That's what you get for crossing Swords with that fellow.'

After that you are ready for anything and may proceed: one at a time, a sentence from à Kempis, a proposition of Euclid. Unnecessary annotation I have tried to avoid – once a note is needed the joke dies – so there may be unavoidable obscurities. It does help to know that a learned and ingenious man called Dunne wrote a book called *An Experiment With Time*; that Tom Moore sang of the bloom of the valley of the Avoca River; that there was a long controversy between London and Dublin over the possession of the Impressionist paintings dubiously bequeathed by the will of Sir Hugh Lane, art dealer and collector, and that the Dublin Municipal Art Gallery, where half the pictures may now be seen (the other half are in the Tate), is in Charlemont House in Parnell

[5] In an occasional poem written in 1913 G. K. Chesterton took the name Swords at its face value in English. The occasion was the seizure by locked out and starving Dublin workers of a herd of cattle in the neighbourhood of the village: a swordlike stroke for liberty. But the name of the place is Sórd Colaim Chille from a pure well (Sórd) said to have been blessed by St Columcille.

Square. Some people too may still remember that Nat Gould wrote novels about the turf; or know that the Arcadia was – may still be – a famous ballroom in the seaside resort of Bray, Co. Wicklow; or know that, in Ireland, to be 'in the Movement' meant to be involved in the 1920s in the ever-with-us struggle for national independence; and that the phrase has acquired, as such phrases may, an ironic connotation. Also: that while the boot is the part of a car that Americans call the trunk, The Boot is a famous pub to the north of Dublin city.

The passage I quote below is an extravagant example of the way in which the column contained matter that must now, since much of the matter of a column is tied to a moment, be meaningless to many who did not know the time, the manners, or the men.

In New York's swank Manhattan lives blond, smiling, plump, James Keats, descendant of the famous poet, John. No lover of poetry, James Keats is director of the million-dollar dairy combine, Manhattan Cheeses, and ranked Number Three in the Gallup Quiz to find America's Ten Ablest Executives. James lives quietly with slim, dark, attractive wife, Anna, knows all there is to know about cheeses, likes a joke like his distinguished forbear. Wife Anna likes to tell of the time he brought her to see the Louis–Baer fight: 'He just sat there roaring – Camembert, Camembert.'
If the joke doesn't interest you [Myles comments], do you derive amusement from this funny way of writing English? It is very smart and up-to-date. It was invented by America's slick glossy *Time* and copied by hacks in every land. For two pins I will write like that every day, in Irish as well as English. Because that sort of writing is taut, meaningful, hard, sinewy, compact, newsy, factual, muscular, meaty, smart, modern, brittle, chromium, bright, flexible, omnispectic.

The passage begins not only as a mockery of the style of *Time* but also as a pointed reference to a then Dublin columnist, a Dutchman, who it was nastily said had learned his English out of that American magazine. It ends in that proliferation of adjectives as a *reductio ad absurdum* of a style that Myles elected to detect in some of the critical articles in the then Dublin literary magazine *The Bell*.

Leafing through *The Irish Times* in pursuit of Keats and Chapman I began for beguilement to make up an adornment for a calendar or desk diary: 'From Myles na Gopaleen – A Thought for Every Day in the Year.' Here are a few; on art, on politics, on life:

'The instinct for propriety and beauty is highly developed even in animals. Hens, for example, are skilled in the plastic arts and can produce works of art that are not only impeccable in design and delicately coloured, but edible.'

Or this about an ultra-republican publication that would now represent the outlook, if that's the word, of some branch of the IRA: 'Your men of *The United Irishman* interpret freedom as a system whereby the fancies of clods are to be imposed by force on everybody.'

Or this, in the mood of an old man in a dry, but mild season: 'Old age, alas! Though it has brought me much... much honour, wealth, a small pension and the admiration of beautiful women...old age has not robbed me of that prime ingredient of romance...the endless capacity for wonder, puzzlement, mild dismay.'

BENEDICT KIELY

The Right Sort of Frog

Many anecdotes have already been recounted bearing on Chapman's conviction that there was easy money in performing animals and the art of the circus. On one occasion he took to training frogs in amphibious ballet but made little progress owing to the diversity of the frogs he caught in size, shape and intelligence. He noticed, however, that it was comparatively easy to frogmarch the small butty type of frogs and commenced breeding this strain.

'I intend to persevere as I am bound to have luck sooner or later,' he remarked to Keats. 'I find it is quite possible to impart knowledge provided one can get the right sort of frog.'

'It's a wrong toad that has no learning,' Keats said.

The Odd Guinea

The medical profession, remember, wasn't always the highly organized racket that it is today. In your grandfather's time practically anybody could take in hand (whatever that means) to be a physician or surgeon and embark on experiments which frequently involved terminating other people's lives. Be that as it may, certain it is that Chapman in his day was as fine a surgeon as ever wore a hat. Chapman took in hand to be an ear, nose and throat man and in many an obscure bedroom he performed prodigies which, if reported in the secular press, would have led to a question in the House. Keats, of course, always went along to pick up the odd guinea that was going for the anaesthetist. Chapman's schoolday lessons in carpentry often saved him from making foolish mistakes.

On one occasion the two savants were summoned to perform a delicate antrum operation. This involved opening up the nasal passages and doing a lot of work in behind the forehead. The deed was done and the two men departed, leaving behind a bleeding ghost suffering severely from what is nowadays called 'post-operative debility'. But through some chance the patient lived through the night, and the following day seemed to have some slim chance of surviving. Weeks passed and there was no mention of his death in the papers. Months passed. Then Chapman got an unpleasant surprise. A letter from the patient containing several pages of abuse, obviously written with a hand that quivered with pain. It appeared that the patient, after 'recovering' somewhat from the operation, developed a painful swelling at the top of his nose. This condition progressed from pain to agony and eventually the patient took to consuming drugs made by his brother, who was a blacksmith. These preparations apparently did more harm than good and the patient had now written to Chapman demanding that he should return and restore the patient's health and retrieve the damage that had been done; otherwise that the brother would call to know the reason why.

'I think I know what is wrong with this person,' Chapman

said. 'I missed one of the needles I was using. Perhaps we had better go and see him.' Keats nodded.

When they arrived the patient could barely speak, but he summoned his remaining strength to utter a terrible flood of bad language at the selfless men who had come a long journey to relieve pain. A glance by the practised eye of Chapman revealed that one of the tiny instruments had, indeed, been sewn up (inadvertently) in the wound, subsequently causing grandiose suppurations. Chapman got to work again, and soon retrieved his property. When the patient was resewn and given two grains, the blacksmith brother arrived and kindly offered to drive the two men home in his trap. The offer was gratefully accepted. At a particularly filthy part of the road, the blacksmith deliberately upset the trap, flinging all the occupants into a morass of muck. This, of course, by way of revenge, accidentally on purpose.

That evening Chapman wore an expression of sadness and depression. He neglected even to do his twenty lines of Homer, a nightly chore from which he had never shrunk in five years.

'To think of the fuss that fellow made over a mere needle, to think of his ingratitude,' he brooded. 'Abusive letters, streams of foul language, and finally arranging to have us fired into a pond full of filth! And all for a tiny needle! Did you ever hear of such vindictiveness!'

'He had it up his nose for you for a long time,' Keats said.

Sherry and Bézique

An ancestor of Keats (by the same token) was concerned in the dread events of the French Revolution. He was, of course, on the aristocratic side, a lonely haughty creature who ignored the ordinances of the rabblement and continued to sit in his Louis Kahn's drawing room drinking pale sherry and playing bézique. Soon, however, he found himself in the cart and was delivered to execution. He surveyed the dread engine of Monsieur Guillotine, assessing its mechanical efficiency and allowing it some small meed of admiration. Then, turning to the executioner, he courteously presented his compliments and prayed that he should be granted a simple favour on the occasion of his last journey – that of being permitted to face away from the guillotine and lean back so that the blade should meet him in the throat rather than that he should adopt the usual attitude of kneeling face down with his neck on the block.

'I like to sit with my back to the engine,' he explained.

Carnival

Keats and Chapman once lived near a church. There was a heavy debt on it. The pastor made many efforts to clear the debt by promoting whist drives and raffles and the like, but was making little headway. He then heard of the popularity of these carnivals where you have swing-boats and round-abouts and fruit-machines and la boule and shooting galleries and every modern convenience. He thought to entertain the town with a week of this and hoped to make some money to reduce the debt. He hired one of these outfits but with his diminutive financial status he could only induce a very third-rate company to come. All their machinery was old and broken. On the opening day, as the steam organ blared forth, the heavens opened and disgorged sheets of icy rain. The scene, with its drenched and tawdry trappings, assumed the gaiety of a morgue. Keats and Chapman waded from stall to stall, soaked and disconsolate. Chapman (unwisely, perhaps) asked the poet what he thought of the fiesta.

'A fête worse than debt,' Keats said.

Chapman collapsed into a trough of mud.

A Thing of Duty

I was thinking (in all seriousness, as the man said) of writing a long paragraph about a man called Reaper who invented a new sort of cushion. This cushion was so far ahead of any other sort of cushion that it revolutionized the whole cushion industry. Having said that much, I had intended to dwell somewhat on the technical aspects of Reaper's invention and then come out with the side-splitting remark that the invention had led to reapercushions throughout the civilized globe. That will give you some idea, Keats once said, apropos of the enduring youthfulness of all policemen, that 'a thing of duty is a boy forever'.

Indeed, I remember once toying with the case of a man who had spent twenty hard years in the service of the Irish Lights Commissioners, mucking around in all sorts of weather with our coastal navigation marks. He met and married a widow who was so wealthy that he found he could retire and live in comfort on her money for the rest of his life. There was some question of him making some remark about being now settled down and having no more nights out with the buoys. All this, as I said, will give you some idea, some inkling of what goes on in my dirty mind. Skip it lug.

Sun-struck Pigeons

When Keats and Chapman were at Greyfriars, the latter manifested a weakness for practical jokes – 'practical jokes' you might call them, indeed, of the oddest kind.

One afternoon Chapman observed the headmaster quietly pacing up and down in the shade of the immemorial elms, completely submerged in Dindorf's *Poetae Scenici Graeci*. It was late summer, and the afternoon stood practically upright on the scorched lawns, weaving drunkenly in its own baked light. Sun-struck pigeons gasped happily in the trees, maggots chuckled dementedly in the grasses, and red ants grimly carried on their interminable transport undertakings. It was very, very hot. Chapman, however, had certain fish to fry and mere heat was not likely to deter him.

He wandered off to an old tool shed and emerged very casually, carrying a small bucket of liquid glue. He took up an unobtrusive position near the pacing headmaster, and waited patiently for his chance. The headmaster approached, turned, and moved again slowly on his way. Instantly Chapman darted out, ran up noiselessly behind the pedagogue, and carefully emptied the bucket of glue all down the back of his coat. In a flash the young joker was back again in the shadow of the elms, carefully studying the results of his work. The headmaster continued his reading, wondering vaguely at the sound of aircraft; for the shining brown mess on the back of his coat had attracted hordes of wasps, bluebottles, gnats, newts, and every manner of dungfly. Chapman from his nook decided that the operation had been successful.

But the end was not yet. Two fifth-form bullies (Snoop and Stott, as it happened) had observed the incident from the distance, and thought it would be funny to turn the tables. They approached Chapman under cover, leaped on him, gagged his mouth, and lifted the little fellow in their arms. The pacing headmaster paced on. When his back was turned, the two fifth-form ruffians ran up behind him, jammed Chapman onto him back to back on the gleaming glue, and were gone before the wretched headmaster had time to realize the extraordinary facts of his situation. That a howling small boy was glued to him high up on his back did not disturb him so much as the murderous punctures of the wasps, who were now angry at being disturbed.

There was hell to pay that evening. Nobody would own up, and every boy in the school was flogged with the exception of Chapman, who was regarded as a victim of the outrage.

After Keats had received his flogging like the rest, he was asked for his opinion of the whole incident, and particularly what he thought of Chapman.

'I like a man that sticks to his principals,' was all he would vouchsafe.

Down the High

Chapman's fag at Greyfriars was a boy called Fox, a weedy absent-minded article of Irish extraction. One evening, shortly before the hour when Mr Quelch was scheduled to take the Remove for prep, the young fellow was sent down the High with a jug and strict instructions to bring back a pint of mild and bitter without spilling it. The minutes lengthened and so did Chapman's face, who disliked going into class completely sober. He fumed and fretted, but still there was no sign of the returning fag. In the opposite arm-chair lay Keats, indolently biting his long nails. He thought he would console his friend with a witty quotation.

'*Fox dimissa nescit reverti,*' he murmured.

'*Dimissus!*' snapped Chapman, always a stickler for that kind of thing.

'Kindly leave my wife out of this,' Keats said stiffly.

On Vesuvius

Keats and Chapman once climbed Vesuvius and stood looking down into the volcano, watching the bubbling lava and considering the sterile ebullience of the stony entrails of the earth. Chapman shuddered as if with cold or fear.

'Will you have a drop of the crater?' Keats said.

A Guinness

Of course there is no drink can compare with a bottle of stout.
It is sui guinnessis. Keats once called a cab and was disgusted
to find the beautiful upholstery ruined with milk spilt by
some previous reveller who had been going home with it.
Instead of crying over the spilt milk, Keats said to the cab-
man: 'What's this? A cabri-au-lait?'

Wehrmacht

Chapman, during his biochemistry days at Munich, had spent years examining and cataloguing all the human glands. He designated each according to a letter of the alphabet, and when he had them all isolated and labelled, he settled down to write a minute medical monograph on each one of them. Gland A, gland B, gland C – Chapman's scholarly dossiers accumulated. Keats looked in to see him one day and found him apparently stumped. One of the glands would not yield to the experiment.

'What's the trouble?' Keats said.

'This gland N,' Chapman replied, 'is giving me a lot of trouble. But I'm going to keep after it. I won't let it beat me. I'll win yet.'

'That's the spirit,' Keats said. Then he began to potter about the place, whistling some tune. Chapman pricked up his ears.

'What's that you're whistling?' he asked.

'Wir fahren gegen N-gland,' Keats said.

Chapman suddenly swallowed some chemical potion he had been working at.

Zurich Tramcars

The 'abstract' painter Franz Huehl, son of a Dresden banker, was living in Zurich eking o. a p. l-hood (like manny a betther man) during the last European war. He was happily married, and his wife, not knowing that young Huehl's allowance had ceased many years ago (in fact when he painted a 'portrait' of his father), was pleased with their comparative prosperity; Huehl – an incorrigible gambler – had had a run of luck at the tables and had won enough to put him on velvet for eighteen months. The wife knew nothing of this. However, the money eventually ran out and, very worried, the young wife went to consult Keats, who at that time was supervising the construction of tramcars for the Zurich Corporation. Keats heard her out. Sympathetic, he determined to tell her the truth.

'My dear girl,' he said, 'you have been living in F. Huehl's pair o'dice.'

When she was gone he turned to Chapman.

'F. Huehl and his Monet are soon parted,' he observed.

Chapman bought the picture next day, for one of his spare lieder.

By the way (whatever that idiot phrase means), we newspaper people often refer laughingly to Schubert as a lieder-writer.

Up a Tree

Chapman once laid out a lot of good money on a mastiff, which the vendor guaranteed to be most friendly, faithful and utterly reliable. Keats, out for a stroll, found his friend shivering up a tree with the beast standing at the bottom uttering fearful menacing growls.

'There's one thing about that dog,' Keats said, 'he's very reliable. He'll never let you down.'

The Manchester School

The poet and Chapman once entered a fine old granite pub in the south of England and got down to some really serious drinking. Keats was in a querulous mood and it was not long till he got into an acrimonious conversation on politics with mine host. The latter was a most irascible character and soon the 'conversation' had developed into a shouting match, the poet's shrill alto overstriding the publican's bass. Chapman tried to make peace but Keats, an unrepentant adherent of the Manchester School, began assailing the publican with foul jibes unheard of in any known lyceum of economics. The publican, shaking with passion, stopped in the middle of his thunderous reply, took up a tumbler and fired it with devastating force at the pale excited poet. It crashed into his windpipe, broke into fragments, and caused terrible throat wounds. Chapman rushed to the poet's aid and soon the two of them were standing outside in the shadow of the grey granite walls, both trying to stifle the spurting gore with sodden handkerchiefs.

'Really, old man,' Chapman said, 'you ought to know that it is unwise to start political arguments in a public house. I'm afraid you were in the wrong.'

'People in stone houses shouldn't throw glasses,' Keats said.

Hatter's Castle

Chapman was once complaining to Keats about the eccentric behaviour of a third party who had rented a desolate stretch of coast and engaged an architect to build a fantastic castle on it. Chapman said that no sane person could think of living in so forsaken a spot, but Keats was more inclined to criticize the rich man on the score of the architect he had chosen, a young man of 'advanced' ideas and negligible experience. Chapman persisted that the site was impossible, and that this third party was a fool.

'His B.Arch. is worse than his bight,' Keats said.

Cats and Dustbins

Chapman, ever in search of new enthusiasms, joined a body known as the Society for the Defence of Civil Liberties. The society financed the grandiose legal battles which individuals undertook in order to secure some private right, such as the right to put cats out at night, to place dustbins on public streets, play musical instruments in congested residential districts, and so forth. An important permanent activity of the society: the review of the propriety, legality, and fairness of taxation, both in substance and in incidence. Its council found that there was ample ground for assailing all taxes, and did so with great ferocity.

The president of the society, in particular, impressed Chapman. He was unremitting in his denunciation of taxation, and had single-handed addressed tens of thousands of letters and telegrams of protest to Government departments. After a rise in Income Tax rates had been announced one year, he solemnly declared that the new taxes would utterly beggar people of his own class, even to the extent of depriving them of essentials such as food and clothing. He bitterly challenged his own assessment and appealed to the Special Commissioners. Time after time he obtained postponements of the hearing on the ground that he had no clothes in which he could appear to make his case. The Commissioners began to lose patience and announced a final date beyond which they would agree to no further postponement. The president of the society on this occasion duly appeared – but attired in a paper suit which he had contrived by taking the offending Finance Act apart and sewing the pages together in the semblance of a jacket and trousers. The appeal was disallowed, but the President's ingenious gesture delighted Chapman, who gave a very long and enthusiastic account of the incident to Keats. The President was, Chapman said, the greatest champion of liberty since Napoleon.

'That fellow's always putting on an Act,' Keats said, drily.

In the Coffin

Keats and Chapman were conversing one day on the street, and what they were conversing about I could not tell you. But anyway there passed a certain character who was renowned far and wide for his piety, and who was reputed to have already made his own coffin, erected it on trestles, and slept in it every night.

'Did you see our friend?' Keats said.

'Yes,' said Chapman, wondering what was coming.

'A terrible man for his bier,' the poet said.

On Tour in France

Chapman once went theatre-mad and started a small fit-up company with which he toured France playing Molière. Keats disapproved of this affectation but went along to take in the money. One night the company was scheduled to perform in a small village a few miles upriver from Paris, where Chapman's small stock of execrable scenery had to be conveyed by barge. There was a frightful accident at the landing stage, all the stuff falling into the water. Chapman burst into tears.

'For once I admire your mise en Seine,' Keats said.

Stradivarius

Keats was once presented with an Irish terrier, which he humorously named Byrne. One day the beast strayed from the house and failed to return at night. Everybody was distressed, save Keats himself. He reached reflectively for his violin, a fairly passable timber of the Stradivarius feciture, and was soon at work with wrist and jaw.

Chapman, looking in for an after-supper pipe, was astonished at the poet's composure, and did not hesitate to say so. Keats smiled (in a way that was rather lovely).

'And why should I not fiddle,' he asked, 'while Byrne roams?'

Arran Banners

When the poet Keats was a lad he was undecided as to his ultimate profession, and spent a few years in business as a potato factor. One day a French noblewoman who was on holiday in the vicinity ordered a ton of Arran Banners. When Keats was delivering the potatoes he was attacked by a ferocious pom, which this lady kept as a pet. The poet presented the pom with the father and the mother of a fair-day kick, and carried on quietly with his work.

'When I make up my mind to deliver spuds,' he remarked afterwards to Chapman, 'I have no intention of letting a pomme de terre me.' Chapman took no notice.

African King

An African potentate, dispossessed of his realm by warlike action, hied to London and took up his quarters in a disused meteorological station, where he managed to continue holding court on a very modest scale. The fortunes of war subsequently changed and he was enabled to land on the shore of his own kingdom from a seaplane. The newspapers recorded that he was received with enthusiastic homage by multitudes of his followers.

It is a safe bet that, if Keats were alive, wild horses and barbed wire would not prevent him from remarking that this was a ruler more honoured on the beach than in the observatory.

The Boots of Cortez

When the poet Keats and his fat friend, Cortez, were doing some exploring work abroad on behalf of the Royal Society, a curious incident took place on the top of a mountain. Stout Cortez had been moody all day, and complained bitterly about his boots during the stiffer part of the climb. When the summit was reached he started looking about him through his glasses. Keats, who was tired, and wanted a smoke, casually tapped the explorer on the arm and asked for a match. He got no reply of any kind. The poet turned with a shrugging gesture to his friend, Chapman.

'Must be huffed,' Chapman remarked.

'In a pique in Darien, in fact,' Keats said.

Coffee for One

Chapman once fell in love and had not been long plying his timid attentions when it was brought to his notice that he had a rival. This rival, a ferocious and burly character, surprised Chapman in the middle of a tender conversation with the lady and immediately challenged him to a duel, being, as he said, prohibited from breaking him into pieces there and then merely by the presence of the lady.

Chapman, who was no duellist, went home and explained what had happened to Keats.

'And I think he means business,' he added. 'I fear it is a case of "pistols for two, coffee for one". Will you be my second?'

'Certainly,' Keats said, 'and since you have the choice of weapons I think you should choose swords rather than pistols.'

Chapman agreed. The rendezvous was duly made and one morning at dawn Keats and Chapman drove in a cab to the dread spot. The poet had taken the 'coffee for one' remark rather too literally and had brought along a small quantity of coffee, sugar, milk, a coffee-pot, a cup, saucer, and spoon, together with a small stove and some paraffin.

After the usual formalities, Chapman and the rival fell to sword-play. The two men fought fiercely, edging hither and thither about the sward. Keats, kneeling and priming the stove, was watching anxiously and saw that his friend was weakening. Suddenly, Chapman's guard fell and his opponent drew back to plunge his weapon home. Keats, with a lightning flick of his arm took up the stove and hurled it at the blade that was poised to kill! With such force and aim so deadly was the stove hurled that it smashed the blade in three places. Chapman was saved!

The affair ended in bloodless recriminations. Chapman was warm in his thanks to Keats.

'You saved my life,' he said, 'by hurling the stove between our blades. You're tops!'

'Primus inter parries,' Keats said.

Meeting of the Waters

Keats and Chapman once paid a visit to the Vale of Avoca, the idea being to have a good look at Moore's tree. Keats brought along his valet, a somewhat gloomy character called Monk. Irish temperament, climate, scenery, and porter did not agree with Monk, whose idea of home and beauty was the East End of London and a glass of mild. He tried to persuade Keats to go home, but the poet had fastened on a local widow and was not to be thwarted by the fads of his servant. Soon it became evident that a breach between them was imminent. Things were brought to a head by a downpour which lasted for three days and nights. Monk tendered a savage resignation, and departed for Dublin in a sodden chaise. The incident annoyed Chapman.

'I think you are well rid of that fellow,' he said. 'He was a sullen lout.'

Keats shook his head despondently.

'The last rays of feeling, and life must depart,' he said sadly, 'ere the bloom of that valet shall fade from my heart.'

Chapman coughed slightly.

Swans on Dog-leads

Once Chapman, in his tireless quest for a way to get rich quick, entered into a contract with a London firm for the supply of ten tons of swansdown. At the time he had no idea where he could get this substance but, on the advice of Keats, went to live with the latter in a hut on a certain river estuary where the rather odd local inhabitants cultivated tame swans for the purposes of their somewhat coarsely grained eggs. Chapman erected several notices in the locality inviting swan-owners to attend at his hut for the purpose of having their fowls combed and offering 'a substantial price' per ounce for the down so obtained.

Soon the hut was surrounded by gaggles of unsavoury-looking natives, each accompanied by four or five disreputable swans on dog-leads. The uproar was enormous and vastly annoyed Keats, who was in bed with toothache. Chapman went out and addressed the multitude and then fell to bargaining with individual owners. After an hour in the pouring rain he came in to Keats, having apparently failed to do business. He was in a vile temper.

'Those appalling louts!' he exploded. 'Why should I go out and humiliate myself before them, beg to be allowed to comb their filthy swans, get soaked to the skin bargaining with them?'

'It'll get you down sooner or later,' Keats mumbled.

On the Tram

Keats (in his day) had a friend named Byrne. Byrne was a rather decent Irish person, but he was frightfully temperamental, politically unstable and difficult to get on with, particularly if the running board of the tram was already crowded with fat women. He frightened the life out of his wife with his odd Marxist ideas.

'What shall I do?' she implored Keats. 'Politics mean nothing to me; his love means much.'

Keats said nothing, but wrote to her that night – 'Please Byrne when Red.'

Boiling Porridge

Chapman had a small cousin whom he wished to put to a trade and he approached Keats for advice. The poet had an old relative who was a tailor and for a consideration this tailor agreed to accept the young man as an apprentice. For the first year, however, he declined to let him do any cutting, insisting that he should first master the art of making garments up.

One day Chapman accidentally spilled some boiling porridge over his only suit, ruining it completely. The same evening he had an appointment with a wealthy widow and was at his wits' end to know how he could get another suit in time. Keats suggested that the young apprentice should be called upon in the emergency. Chapman thought this a good idea and sent the apprentice an urgent message. Afterwards he had some misgivings as to the ability of a mere apprentice to produce a wearable suit in a few hours.

'He'll certainly want to spare no effort to have it finished by six o'clock,' he said gloomily.

'He'll have his work cut out,' Keats said reassuringly.

Some Dread Disease

Keats and Chapman once called to see a titled friend and after the host had hospitably produced a bottle of whiskey, the two visitors were called into consultation regarding the son of the house, who had been exhibiting a disquieting redness of face and boisterousness of manner at the age of twelve. The father was worried, suspecting some dread disease. The youngster was produced but the two visitors, glass in hand, declined to make any diagnosis. When leaving the big house, Chapman rubbed his hands briskly and remarked on the cold.

'I think it must be freezing and I'm glad of that drink,' he said. 'By the way, did you think what I thought about that youngster?'

'There's a nip in the heir,' Keats said.

A Monkish Garment

Here is a good one.

Keats and Chapman, overtaken by a snowstorm when on a journey, were compelled to repair to an inferior inn. After a musty repast, the landlord conducted them to an attic where one iron bed was indicated as the lair of both for the night. Protests were useless, and the two travellers undressed and tried to sleep. The bed-linen was of the meagrest and both soon discovered that they were being frozen to death. Chapman suggested that they should have recourse to the extra weight of their dressing gowns. Keats agreed. Both men rose. As Chapman was engaged in arranging his dressing gown as an impromptu coverlet, he noticed that Keats had donned his (a cinctured and very monkish garment) and was already getting back into bed.

'You don't mean to say that you are going to wear your dressing gown in bed?' Chapman said testily, knowing he was being robbed of his share of it. 'That is surely a most reprehensible practice!'

'It's a bed habit,' Keats said.

Empty Heaven

Chapman was much given to dreaming and often related to Keats the strange things he saw when in bed asleep. On one occasion he dreamt that he had died and gone to heaven. He was surprised and rather disappointed at what he saw for although the surroundings were most pleasant, there seemed to be nobody about. The place seemed to be completely empty and Chapman saw himself wandering disconsolately about looking for somebody to talk to. He suddenly woke up without solving this curious puzzle.

'It was very strange,' he told Keats. 'I looked everywhere but there wasn't a soul to be seen.'

Keats nodded understandingly.

'There wasn't a sinner in the place,' he said.

Wild Sheep

Chapman once took to sheep-farming, renting a large mountain for the purpose. Soon he had a herd of about five hundred sheep at pasture on it. After a time he began to suspect that local people were stealing the sheep and selling them at distant fairs. He then tried to brand the sheep so that they could be recognized but the sheep were wild and he failed to catch any save one, a lame and diseased specimen. This he let go again and went to Keats for advice. Keats advised that several scratching posts should be erected in various parts of the bare mountain and that the posts should be coated with a perpetually moist sort of paint which he himself promised to prepare. The sheep would thus brand themselves within a week.

Chapman was pleased with this ingenious scheme and adopted it immediately. Soon he had the posts erected and very shortly afterwards any of the sheep that came in view were observed to be generously marked with red paint. The thieves were evidently foiled and Chapman was loud in his praise of the poet.

But one day the pair were at a local fair and Chapman was surprised to see the lame sheep he had once caught offered for sale by a very shifty-eyed character. The beast was unmarked.

'I know for a fact that that beast is mine,' Chapman said to Keats, 'but it's hardly worth raising a row about it as it is diseased and deformed and out of place in my thoroughbred flock.'

'It didn't come up to scratch,' Keats said.

Warts

One winter's evening Keats looked up to find Chapman regarding him closely. He naturally enquired the reason for this scrutiny.

'I was thinking about those warts on your face,' Chapman said.

'What about them?' the poet said testily.

'Oh, nothing,' Chapman said. 'It just occurred to me that you might like to have them removed.'

'They are there for years,' Keats said, 'and I don't see any particular reason for getting worried about them now.'

'But they are rather a blemish,' Chapman persisted. 'I wouldn't mind one – but four fairly close together, that's rather—'

'Four?' Keats cried. 'There were only three there this morning!'

'There are four there now,' Chapman said.

'That's a new one on me,' Keats said.

The Delights of Bray

It is not generally known that two years in succession Chapman spent his summer holidays in Bray, Co. Wicklow. He was at that time a young man and had not yet met Keats, the poet with whom his name was fated ever to be linked. He spent most of his nights dancing and enjoying himself enormously. These holidays were such pleasant memories afterwards that he never tired of telling his friends about them and praising Bray. Indeed, on the occasion of his first meeting with Keats, he asked the poet whether he had ever visited this delightful Irish watering place. Keats said that he had.

'I am delighted to hear it,' Chapman said enthusiastically, 'I think Bray is wonderful. When I was there I went mad about dancing and spent night after night in the Arcadia ballroom. I thought the floor was one of the best I had ever encountered and all the ladies I met there were expert dancers. I enjoyed myself immensely. Why, I practically *lived* there! Do you know the place yourself?'

'*Et ego in Arcadia vixi*,' Keats said wearily.

And Heidelberg

While Keats and Chapman were at Heidelberg arranging for the purchase of cheap doctorates, the latter conceived a violent, wholly mysterious attachment for a practically supernumerary lecturer in Materia Med., by name Jakob Arnim-Woelkus, an incredible bore and a man wanting in the meanest of personal accomplishments. Chapman never wearied of this person's company and, in his absence, was forever retailing the 'pleasantries' and sophisms of the deplorable bore. Keats, who could not bear this, kept out of his compatriot's way as much as possible. Late in term, however, Keats, to heal the scars he had received in a duel, went walking into the mountains and persuaded Chapman to accompany him, fearing less the devil he knew than any foreigner. The two walked for hours, Keats gloomy, Chapman meditative. Not a word was exchanged till eventually they came to the brow of a hill whence a fine landscape was to be seen.

Chapman, moved, spoke, student-wise, in dog-Latin: 'Ah, Keats! *Hic utinam nunc sit Jacobus Arnim-Woelkus, doctor praeclarissimus noster!*' Keats snarled.

'*Odi*,' he roared, '*odi Prof. Arnim-Woelkus!*'

The Battle of Ventry

Keats and Chapman met one Christmas Eve and fell to comparing notes on the Christmas present each had bought himself. Keats had bought himself a ten-glass bottle of whiskey and paid thirty shillings for it in the black market.

'That is far too dear,' Chapman said. 'Eighteen shillings is plenty to pay for a ten-glass bottle.'

Chapman then explained that he had bought a valuable Irish manuscript, one of the oldest copies of the Battle of Ventry, or *Cath Fionntragha*. He explained that the value of the document was much enhanced by certain interlineal Latin equivalents of obscure Irish words.

'How many such interlineal comments are there?' Keats asked.

'Ten,' Chapman said.

'And how much did you pay for this thing?' Keats asked.

'Forty-five shillings,' Chapman said defiantly.

'Eighteen shillings is plenty to pay for a ten-gloss battle,' Keats said crankily.

Rare China

A millionaire collector (whose name was ever associated with that old-time Irish swordsman of France, O'Shea d'Ar) once invited Chapman and Keats to dinner. The invitation came quite at the wrong time for Keats, who was crippled with stomach trouble. Chapman insisted, however, that the poet should come along and endeavour to disguise his malady, holding that millionaires were necessarily personable folk whose friendship could be very beautiful. Keats was too ill to oppose Chapman's proposal and in due course found himself in a cab bound for the rich man's bounteous apartments.

On arrival Chapman covered up his friend's incapacity by engaging the host in loud non-stop conversations and also managed to have Keats placed at an obscure corner of the table where little notice would be taken of him. Slumped in his chair, the unfortunate poet saw flunkeys deposit course after course before him but beyond raking his knife and fork in desultory attempts to make a show of eating, he did not touch it.

When the main course was served – a sight entirely disgusting to the eye of Keats – Chapman and the host were in the middle of a discussion on rare china. The host directed that a valuable vase on the mantelpiece should be passed round to the guests for inspection. Chapman gave a most enthusiastic dissertation on it, identifying it as a piece of the Ming dynasty. He then passed it to Keats, who was still slumped over his untouched platter of grub. The poet had not been following the conversation and apparently assumed that Chapman was trying to aid him in his extremity. He muttered something about the vase being 'a godsend' and after a moment handed it to the flunkey to be replaced on the mantelpiece. On the way home that evening Chapman violently reproached his friend for not making a fuss about the vase and pleasing the host.

'I saw nothing very special about it,' Keats said.

'Good heavens man,' Chapman expostulated, 'it was a

priceless Ming vase, worth thousands of pounds! Why didn't you at least say nothing if you couldn't say something suitable?'

'I'm afraid I put my food in it,' Keats said.

Festina Lente

Keats once tried to collar the Christmas card trade in pretty mottoes. He bought a quantity of small white boards and got to work burning philosophical quotations on them with a tiny poker. *Festina Lente*, *Carpe Diem* and *Dum Spiro Spero*, were produced in great numbers. Becoming more ambitious, the poet showed Chapman a board bearing the words *Proximus Ardet Ucalegon*.

'One does not like to be captious,' Chapman said, 'but I'm afraid there's a word left out there.'

Keats looked at the board again.

'You want *Jam* on it,' he said.

At Charing Cross

In his earlier and less prosperous days Keats was compelled to take employment as a ticket-checker at Charing Cross. One day a drunken traveller staggered out of a train, found his ticket only after lengthy rummaging, and by way of recompense for the delay invited the poet across the road for a pint of mild. Keats, aristocrat that he was, would not have said no to medher of Mediterranean brandy, but he resented the coarse invitation to swill beer with this eczemic sot.

'Why should you think I drink beer?' he demanded hotly.

'Beggars can't be choosers,' said the traveller.

'And checkers can't be boozers,' said Keats, turning on his heel.

Mention of Keats reminds me of the death of the elder Poincaré. He was abed and in white torment at the thought that the wealth he had amassed would be dissipated gleefully by his wild sons, whom he had always kept on a tight rein and refused even a ride on the new-fangled motor cars.

'Après moi le Delage!' was his last utterance.

A Greek Colony

Keats and Chapman, shortly after they had taken out their BAs, flung themselves with great enthusiasm into the excitement of practical archaeology. They fitted out a modest personal expedition to a country in the outskirts of Mycenae, which had received much attention from preceding explorers. The ground was regarded as fairly well 'worked out', the indications having been that it was the abode of an early Greek colony. Keats and Chapman were the objects of much derision for their presumptuousness in choosing such a location for their 'prentice dig. They were undeterred, however, and started vigorous excavations.

In a few weeks they encountered, much to their excitement, a large underground chamber which had all the appearance of a primitive burial place. After further work they descended into the apartment and found several corpses which were embalmed and clothed in elaborate garments. Chapman paused to inspect one body; that of an elderly soldierly-looking man with a clipped grey moustache. He called out to Keats very excitedly and drew his attention to the fact that the man's garments were all stitched and fitted to the figure, unlike the loose, draped attire of the Greeks.

'This is a pre-Hellenic colony!' he cried. 'These were the original inhabitants of the country! This man...this man must be 3,500 years old!'

Keats thoughtfully regarded the trim figure.

'He doesn't look half his age,' he said. 'He's very well preserved.'

Wedding Presents

Keats had a young lady cousin who called one day to inform him that a romance she had been conducting for some years had finally flowered and that himself and his friends were invited to the wedding. The poet knew that this meant a present and accepted the invitation with the utmost reluctance. He decided, however, to extend the invitation to Chapman in the hope that the latter would weigh in with a present so impressive that the poet's own miserable gift would be overlooked. Chapman was delighted at the prospect of being a wedding guest.

'It will mean a present,' Keats reminded him nervously.

'Of course,' Chapman said cheerfully. 'That's why I like going to weddings. You see, I make my own presents. It is so much more...personal.'

This was very unpleasant news for the poet, who now saw every prospect of having even his own gift exceeded in wretchedness by the unthinkable homemade article that Chapman was threatening to produce.

After a week Chapman called bearing a small elongated parcel. He placed it with ceremony on the table.

'At this wedding of your cousin's,' he said, 'I presume they will have the usual multi-tiered iced cake?'

'I believe so,' Keats said nervously.

'Good. I have something here that they'll find very useful.'

Chapman then opened the parcel and produced an atrocious homemade 'knife'. The handle appeared to have been made from an old bicycle pump, while the 'blade', attached by a mess of glue, looked like part of a lawn-mower, the whole covered with a cheap silver paint. Though expecting the worst, Keats was astounded at the crudeness of this 'present' and could not see that it could be redeemed by a present on his own part of anything less than a grand piano. He groaned and ran his fingers over the 'blade'. Chapman's eyes were dancing with pride and delight.

'Do you think they will be very impressed with it?' he asked lightly.

'It won't cut any ice,' Keats said glumly.

In the Highlands

Keats and Chapman once spent a holiday in the highlands of Scotland. Keats wanted to buy a tame deer and said something about 'my hart's in the highlands', but that's not what I want to talk about. They were trying to manage on the cheap, sharing everything to keep down costs. Keats even insisted that they should share one horse on their daily travels, which was carrying things (to wit himself and Chapman) a bit far. When they got back to London Keats was asked how he had fared with Chapman. The poet explained that Chapman was a very difficult man to get on with.

(Because the horse was so small, of course.)

The Coiner

Keats had a nephew who evinced, even in early childhood, an unusual talent for manufacturing spurious coins. At the age of twelve he was already in the habit of making his own pocket money. His parents were poor and could not procure for him the tuition that would enable him to proceed from the science of penny-making to the more intricate and remunerative medium of work in silver. The boy's attempts at making half-crowns were very poor indeed and on one occasion resulted in the father being presented with six months' hard labour by a local magistrate. Keats, who was in reduced circumstances and could not offer any help himself, put the problem before Chapman, who was in tow with a wealthy widow. The widow was induced to give £100 to have the boy educated. Six months after the money had been given over and a tutor found, Keats and Chapman visited the boy's home to see what progress was being made. They found the boy in his workshop engrossed in the production of a very colourable half-crown, working with meticulous industry on what was a very lifelike representation of his late Majesty, King Edward. To Keats, Chapman expressed satisfaction at the improvement in the boy's skill.

'I think he is making excellent progress,' he said.

'He is forging ahead,' Keats said.

A Man Called Dunne

Keats once met a man called Dunne and invited him to dinner. It happened that Dunne was a hefty, well-nourished party who usually ordered his steaks in pairs and spent at least two hours at the table every time he visited it. He accepted the poet's invitation and was thunderstruck to find himself faced with a mess of green herbs, with damn the thing else to relieve the green greenness of it all.

'What's this?' he asked rudely.

'An experiment with thyme,' Keats said.

Chapman's Bears

Some time after the well-known occasion when Chapman and Hall had a row and the partnership dissolved, Chapman found himself in rather poor circumstances and looked round for some means of making a living. Through the kindness of a friend, he got an option on two performing bears and managed to buy them cheap. He began to tour the country with these animals and naturally insisted that Keats should go along as a general factotum.

Keats was very scared of the bears and would not accept Chapman's assurance that they were tame and harmless. He refused to go within hugging distance and it was with ill grace that he performed his duties of collecting slops to feed them. One day Chapman was laid up with a fever and he instructed Keats to put the bears through the usual nightly performance, pointing out that it would not do to cancel the performance. Keats neither agreed nor refused but merely went out. Later, from his window, Chapman could see people streaming as usual into the marquee. Nevertheless, he felt suspicious. He managed to drag on his clothes and staggered down to the tent.

He found the bears sitting up on boxes, licking their lips and moving their heads but otherwise remaining as still as statues. Keats could be seen behind them, injecting huge quantities of fluid into their spines with a veterinary surgeon's hypodermic. It transpired that the poet had rendered the bodies of the animals completely numb by means of bucketfuls of local anaesthetic. Chapman flew into a feverish temper and demanded the reason for this brutal and cynical outrage.

'There's safety in numb bears,' Keats said.

A Bite of Supper

Keats had a weakness for doing the gallant but his meanness in money matters often detracted from the largeness of a hospitable gesture. On one occasion he did the stage-door johnny and invited a chorus girl home to his rooms for 'a bite of supper' (which in those days was taken to mean a cold fowl and champagne). The lady consented. She was not very pleased, however, when she discovered that the poet was doing things on the cheap and had laid in merely a quantity of cooked ham and a dozen Bass. She picked diffidently at the ham and did her sulky best with one bottle of the beer. The poet opened his own bottle, whipped off one of the lady's dainty little shoes, filled it till there were beaded bubbles winking at the brim, and then with a gallant ' *Santé!* ' began to drink.

He drank bottle after bottle in this fashion while the lady produced a private flask of drugged cognac and began to get herself well and truly plastered. The evening wore on (curiously enough). The poet's diminutive stomach rebelled after a time and he had the greatest difficulty in swallowing bottle number ten. By this time the lady was practically asleep. The hiccupping poet filled her shoe with the eleventh bottle but suddenly realizing that the last tram was due and that he would be stuck for a taxi if the lady missed it, he put the brimming shoe on the floor, rammed her foot into it, and started to drag her hastily down the stairs and out into the street. She staggered along gamely on his arm and who should the pair encounter only Chapman making his way home. Chapman was alarmed at the girl's appearance.

'What's wrong with your friend?' he asked. 'She is lame.'
'She has an ale in her shoe,' Keats said.

Dentistry

When Keats was practising as a dentist (remember my old joke about abscess makes the heart grow fonder?) a somewhat nervous patient called to have two teeth extracted. Keats assured him that it would not be safe to use a local anaesthetic owing to the extent of suppuration. The patient did not like the idea of a general anaesthetic. He enquired what it was proposed to put him to sleep with.

'I will give you three gases,' Keats said.

Lions

The poet and Chapman once visited a circus. Chapman was very impressed by an act in which lions were used. A trainer entered a cage in which were two ferocious-looking specimens, sat down unconcernedly, took out a paper, and began to read.

'He's reading between the lions,' Keats said.

Bombay Harbour

(Readers are warned that this is extra special; if you don't get it, you probably have a permanent cold in the head – high up.)

Keats and Chapman were entrusted by the British Government with a secret mission which involved a trip to India. A man-of-war awaited them at a British port. Leaving their lodgings at dawn, they were driven at a furious pace to the point of embarkation. When about to rush on board, they encountered at the dockside a mutual friend, one Mr Childs, who chanced to be there on business connected with his calling of wine importer. Perfunctory and very hasty courtesies were exchanged; Keats and Chapman then rushed on board the man-of-war, which instantly weighed anchor. The trip to India was made in the fastest time then heard of, and as soon as the ship had come to anchor in Bombay harbour, the two friends were whisked to land in a wherry. Knowing that time was of the essence of their mission, they hastened from the docks into the neighbouring streets and on turning a corner, whom should they see only——

Mr Childs? No.

Just a lot of Indians, complete strangers.

'Big world,' Keats remarked.

Hats and Leggings

A niece of Chapman's having become engaged to be married, he consulted Keats on matters of etiquette and protocol arising out of the wedding. Keats insisted that all relatives must be asked to the reception, but Chapman demurred, explaining that the bride had an impossible uncle who manufactured felt hats and leggings in a back-street factory in a town in Yorkshire. This man was uncouth, notoriously mean, but above all an arrogant, domineering type whose presence at any social gathering inevitably led to trouble and even blows. Keats was adamant, saying that the exclusion of any near relative, however objectionable, might lead to bitter family quarrels; in any event, he added, the man had money. This latter remark somewhat mollified Chapman.

'If he's asked to come,' he said, 'he'll certainly throw his weight around but on the other hand he may be goaded by the romantic occasion into bringing costly gifts, notwithstanding his reputation in that regard.'

Keats gave a wintry smile.

'I imagine he'll make his presents felt,' he said.

Steel

Keats and Chapman were invited to view the wonders of a steel rolling mill and gratefully accepted the invitation. They watched with awe the giant hammers and rollers moulding crude steel into hawsers, plates and bars. The poet was so fascinated by this that he did not notice that a travelling overhead hook had caught Chapman by the coat and yanked him away through a sinister aperture in the brickwork; nor did he perceive, either, the subsequent crash and sound of muffled screams. He was thus astounded to be shown Chapman later seated in the firm's first aid station, a bloody spectacle whose anatomical attitude suggested broken bones.

'What on earth happened you?' Keats demanded.

The injured man made some attempt to reply but his jaws were smashed and his words could not be heard. His effort to speak, however, was a serious strain and he instantly fainted.

'He looks as if he has been through the mill,' Keats remarked to a frightened bystander.

Chapman's Castle

Once upon a time Chapman inherited a large mountain estate which contained a derelict castle and was reputed to contain unknown quantities of wild sheep and deer. Keats advised his friend to sell the place immediately, as the castle was uninhabitable, sheep-farming was too speculative – particularly for an amateur – and in any case he (Keats) was in need of ready money.

The suggestion angered Chapman, who was very proud of having become a landowner. He icily explained to Keats a unique scheme he had devised for operating the estate profitably by gathering and selling the long wool of the wild sheep. He would employ men to sprinkle an itch powder all over the bushes and gorse on the mountainside; he would then erect hundreds of spiked scratching poles; the sheep, he said, demented by the irritation of the powder, would rub off most of their wool on these poles; the wool would then be collected in sacks and quickly marketed at a profit of four to five thousand pounds. Keats denounced this plan as 'wool-gathering' and the two friends parted after a bitter scene, Chapman going off to live in his castle.

About a month afterwards Keats won a prize of £1,000 in a lottery and used part of the money to satisfy his burning resentment against Chapman's selfish behaviour. He penetrated by night to the boundaries of the estate and in several places cut the wire fencing so that Chapman's animals (if any) would escape. Some weeks later, Chapman, having heard of his friend's windfall, visited him in an apologetic and conciliatory mood and after some rather stilted talk, asked for the loan of £500 'as working capital'.

'You must be crazy,' Keats said, 'if you think I'm going to put money into that wool business.'

'I've given that idea up,' Chapman said.

'Because the sheep didn't come up to scratch?'

'Yes,' Chapman admitted. 'My new plan is to trap the deer on the estate and sell the hides.'

'What security would I have for my money?' Keats asked.

'The deer that we capture,' Chapman said.

'Nobody would lend you a penny on that basis,' Keats said.

Chapman was aghast.

'A good stag,' he cried, 'would be worth at least fifty pounds. If it has no value as security...then...I haven't got a leg to stand on?'

Keats laughed hollowly.

'I happen to know,' he said, 'that you haven't a stag for me to lend on!'

Chapman nearly fainted.

'And furthermore,' Keats continued savagely, 'I intend to keep any doe I may have for my own use!'

Man of Music

Keats and Chapman, wintering on the Continent in a palmy period, met by chance a very talented musician who was in the last stages of destitution and degradation from the consumption of potent drugs. Keats instantly perceived that the man was a master violinist, a composer of immense possibilities and, incidentally, no mean hand with the paint-brush. A veritable sponge of nature if there ever was one. Keats arranged that this great man should enter a nursing home and undertake a course of rehabilitation. The bold plan worked. After some months the man of genius had recovered his health, though his restored vitality gave evidence that he was by nature a very irascible character. His repeated expressions of thanks to Keats and Chapman were punctuated by terrible paroxysms of wrath, denunciations of other musicians, and demands for money. Keats wisely divined that the great man was secretly irked by what he took to be charity, and that his personality would be corrected and fortified if he were made, so to speak, the architect of his own regeneration. With this in mind, the poet approached the management of a well-known *Staatsoper* (which shall be nameless) and paid over a large sum of money on condition that the man of music should be employed as conductor of the orchestra at a large salary.

And so it was done. The members of the orchestra were quick to perceive the great talents of their new master, and complied with his least whim in most obsequious fashion. They had to unlearn all former styles of play and dedicate themselves to uniquely new modes of musical thought. Their humble anxiety to please, however, earned for them only torrents of insult and abuse from the conductor. He stamped, stormed and raved, and frequently walked out of rehearsals pale with rage. No matter how minutely the players obeyed his instructions, the result was the same. Disorder led to chaos and eventually four of the first fiddlers rebelled. A strike was called, and the management explained to Keats that his protégé, however immensely gifted, was impossible. His employment would have to terminate.

Keats and Chapman walked moodily home through the winter snows. Chapman sympathized with the poet on the question of the latter's wasted money and blasted hopes.

'He's an ungrateful so-and-so,' he said, 'and a fool to bite the hand that feeds him.'

'He's a fool,' Keats said bitterly, 'to fight the band that heeds him.'

Chapman accidentally fell down a grating at this stage.

The X-Ray Eye

In their leaner days Keats and Chapman were reduced to making a living in the halls. Chapman had invented a fortune-telling device operated by a one-horsepower electric motor. He called this machine 'The X-Ray Eye'. It was – as were most baffling gadgets in those days – worked with mirrors. Inside the 'electric eye' was set a very strong electric bulb which cast, through the lenses of the 'eye', a penetrating shaft of light through the darkened auditorium. Inside the eye and opposite the machine was a little screen upon which various character-reading words such as 'GENEROUS', 'WARM-HEARTED', 'BRAINY' could be made to appear one at a time by the mere turn of a handle. By manipulating the handle and turning the universally jointed eye hither and thither about the auditorium, Chapman could make the magnified reflection of these mottoes appear in blazing letters on the chests of members of the audience. Naturally the words were altered to suit the taste of local audiences. It was Keats's task to attend to this but on one occasion he neglected to make the change with the result that the unsuspecting Chapman appeared one night before a refined London audience with mottoes which had been in use in Lancashire. First time the 'eye' fixed on a most respectable captain of industry, who saw – to a horror that was no less than Chapman's – that the word 'DRUNKARD' was engraved by the 'eye' on his boiled shirt. The outraged citizen leapt to his feet, shook his fist at Chapman, protested furiously, and began to call for the manager. The situation was saved by Keats.

'He's casting no reflections on you,' he called out from a box.

From Readers

Nearly all the Keats stories which reach me from outside are, for one reason or another, pretty bad. They are bad in the sense that they are too good, too polished and refined, too 'worked over', as Seán Ó Faoláin would say. They lack effervescence and spontaneity. They are 'literary'. They are too obviously contrived and usually omit the essential boredom of the build-up.

Let me cite an example.

Keats once upon a time became an aviator. When he was up in the skies on a certain day, two young fighter pilots began to 'buzz' him. They began flying unnecessarily close alongside, rolled over him and under him, and eventually put his nerves into a terrible condition. He began to think that every minute was his last. He was flying a heavy bomber and had no chance to outmanoeuvre his adversaries.

Chapman, who was at the airport, anxiously scanned the skies. He noticed that the machine piloted by Keats suddenly seemed to stop. The nervous pilot had apparently by accident cut out the four motors.

The two fighter pilots, taking fright at what they had done, veered off. Keats managed to get his own engines going again and in due course made a perfect three-point landing. Chapman hurried over to the poet.

'Indecision is a very dangerous thing when you are flying a bomber,' he said. 'What happened to you up there?'

'I was stalling between two fools,' Keats said curtly.

ANOTHER

You see? Smart, cute, but not really funny. Now read this following one fabricated by me personally:

Keats and Chapman were hired by a State department as detectives to find out whether a certain steel rolling mill was complying with the safety regulations. They were given the standard instruction to all spies: 'We will pay you if you get the information but, if you are caught, expect no recognition from us.'

Duly they penetrated into the works, disguised as apprentices.

While Chapman was walking across a workshop, some careless labourer made a mistake. A steel cable whipped across the floor, struck Chapman, and beheaded him.

Keats ran to his assistance. His early experience as an embryo doctor stood him in good stead. He retrieved Chapman's head, produced needle and suture, and inside ten minutes had sewn on the head again.

In due course Chapman came to, was still a bit dazed, and asked for a cigarette.

'What happened?' he asked.

'Part of you was cut off by a cable,' Keats whispered.

'What part?' Chapman asked.

'Your head,' Keats confided, 'but keep it under your hat.'

You see the difference?

Drunken Driving

Chapman once bought an expensive car and invited Keats to come for a drive. The poet accepted, and installed himself in grand style in the back. After a time he asked Chapman to pull up for a drink. Chapman refused firmly on the ground that drinking and driving were incompatible, that he himself was a fast driver, and that even one drink would be dangerous. His reply was received in complete silence. Wondering whether Keats was offended, he glanced back and was astounded to see that this friend was missing. Although the speed had been about sixty miles an hour, Chapman stopped, turned the car, and went back, thinking that Keats had taken a suicidal leap from the vehicle. But there was no sign of an injured poet on the road. Completely mystified, Chapman continued on his journey, and, after some miles, was flabbergasted to hear the suave voice of his friend commenting favourably on certain Jersey cows in a field.

'If I may ask a question,' Chapman stammered, 'where have *you* been?'

'I was out having a drink in The Boot,' Keats said.

(TECHNICAL NOTE: In many modern cars there is access to the luggage compartment from within.)

A Millionaire

Chapman on one occasion was commissioned by an enormously wealthy businessman to advise on wallpapers for the state rooms of a yacht then building. The millionaire was however unbelievably busy and could talk to Chapman only in his luxurious car on the ten-minute journey between mansion and office. At first Chapman, being well paid for his pains, did not mind this exiguous procedure but as time passed a number of unknown advisers on other matters were picked up at various corners so that on some mornings the car was packed with up to eight people simultaneously giving the fur-coated boss very expensive advice. This amazed Chapman enormously, as he was failing completely to make himself heard on wallpaper schemes. The last straw was provided one morning when the car, packed to the roof with babbling experts, was joined by a mysterious lawyer, who stood outside on the running board of the racing vehicle pouring advice in through the window. This happened several mornings in succession, and Chapman eventually complained bitterly to Keats.

'That solicitor should be struck off the Rolls,' Keats said.

Gardeners

The following is the work of a reader:

Keats and Chapman once worked as gardeners on a big estate, Keats being in charge of flowers, and Chapman in charge of the drives and their adjoining lines of box, laurel, and privet.

It was the habit of the owner of this estate to give a prize annually to the neatest gardener, and it was with great satisfaction that Chapman once obtained this trophy, especially as he was contesting with Keats for the attention of a comely servant girl.

The day following the presentation of the award, Chapman was pinning a rosette, indicating he had won, to a tree bordering the main drive, when he slipped off a ladder. Just previous to this, he had noticed Keats and the maid approaching, so in order that they might not see his predicament, he remained quiet where he had fallen on the thick evergreens.

When the pair passed, they noticed him, and the girl asked Keats what Chapman was doing on the bushes, having not noticed him fall.

'He's resting on his laurels,' the poet said.

Chapman in Love

One evening Keats, working quietly at his books, was devastated by an inundation of Chapman. The poet's friend was distended with passion, inarticulate, a man driven mad by jealousy. When given a drink and pacified, he related the events which led to his condition. To a lady of the most ravishing beauty he had lost his heart; his sentiment was warmly reciprocated, and an early marriage was all that remained to perfect his bliss. Quite suddenly, however, a lout of an artist who specialized in ladies' portraits arrived upon the scene, begged to be permitted to paint the lady, and was granted this boon by the unthinking lover. His chagrin and rage may be guessed when it is revealed that the rascally artist forthwith laid siege to the lady's heart – with not inconsiderable results. After a time she ceased to be in when Chapman called with flowers; on two occasions she had been seen boating with this artist.

'I am beside myself,' Chapman cried, beating his head, 'and so far as I can see only two courses are open to me. I must either take my razor and slit that wretched fellow's throat from ear to ear – that or terminate completely my association with her!'

Keats considered the problem in silence for a considerable time. Finally he spoke:

'If I were you,' he said, 'I'd cut the painter.'

Espionage

During one of the wars Keats and Chapman, having a distaste for service in the conventional (and indeed dangerous) sense, placed their persons at the disposal of a certain power in the capacity of secret service agents. Their offer was accepted, though with some misgiving, and their first assignment involved the purchase or theft of certain secret ordnance maps of Denmark. Both men were provided with considerable sums in foreign currencies and covertly set off for certain centres of Continental intrigue. Chapman in due course contacted a member of the political underworld, discreetly revealed that he required certain maps and that money was no object. Keats did not favour his rather overt manner of doing business and, moreover, suspected the *bona fides* of the rascally-looking foreigner. Chapman, however, was not to be dissuaded.

The foreigner swore he could produce a complete set of maps: he mentioned a price but required half the money in advance since he in turn would also have to pay. Chapman, convinced that he was on a winner, paid, and it was agreed that the rendezvous should be a certain quiet restaurant. Chapman intimated that he would stand dinner to celebrate the conclusion of the transaction but the foreigner protested that the privilege should be his: he would, in fact, order a sumptuous dinner in advance since the *maître* was his personal friend. For his own part he might be slightly late in arriving but it would be unfair to the food that his two guests should delay in starting.

Keats and Chapman arrived at the appointed hour and were served with a glass of sherry followed by a very inferior egg dish. This appeared to constitute the 'sumptuous dinner', since no attempt was made to serve anything further. The two friends, uncertain now as to whether they had been poisoned, sat disconsolately and smoked as the hours went by.

'It is too bad,' Chapman said at last. 'The money gone, a

glass of wine and one wretched dish in exchange, and no maps. And no sign of our friend…'

'It is omelette without the prints of Denmark,' Keats said glumly.

Mineral Wealth

It is not generally known that...

O excuse me.

Keats and Chapman (in the old days) spent several months in the county Wicklow prospecting for ochre deposits. That was before the days of (your) modern devices for geological divination. With Keats and Chapman it was literally a question of smelling the stuff out. The pair of them sniffed their way into Glenmalure and out of it again, and then snuffled back to Woodenbridge. In a field of turnips near Avoca Keats suddenly got the pungent effluvium of a vast ochre mine and lay for hours face down in the muck delightedly permeating his nostrils with the perfume of hidden wealth. No less lucky was Chapman. He had nosed away in the direction of Newtownmountkennedy and came racing back shouting that he too had found a mine. He implored Keats to come and confirm his nasal diagnosis. Keats agreed. He accompanied Chapman to the site and lay down in the dirt to do his sniffing. Then he rose.

'Great mines stink alike,' he said.

Burning Calf

Once when Keats was rotting in Paris a kind old lady gave him a lump of veal and advised him to go home and cook and stuff it into himself. During a desperate attempt to grill it with tongs over an open fire, the meat caught alight.

The poet is thought to have muttered something like 'la Veal lumière' (under breath that hinted of bountifullest barleycorn). Chapman was out at the Folies.

Eugenics and Horseplay

Chapman once became immersed in the study of dialectical materialism, particularly insofar as economic and sociological planning could be demonstrated to condition eugenics, birth rates, and anthropology. His wrangles with Keats lasted far into the night. He was particularly obsessed by the fact that in the animal kingdom, where there was no self-evident plan of ordered society and where connubial relations were casual and polygamous, the breed prospered and disease remained of modest dimensions. Where there was any attempt at the imposition from without – and he instanced the scientific breeding of race-horses by humans – the breed prospered even more remarkably. He was not slow to point out that philosophers of the school of Marx and Engels had ignored the apparent necessity for ordered breeding on the part of humans as a concomitant to planning in the social and economic spheres. Was this, he once asked Keats, to be taken as evidence of superior reproductive selection on the part of, say horses – or was it to be taken that a man of the stamp of Engels deliberately shirked an issue too imponderable for rationative evaluation?

The poet found this sort of thing boring, and frowned.

'Foals rush in where Engels feared to tread,' he said morosely.

Runaway Gelding

Keats, when living in the country, purchased an expensive chestnut gelding. This animal was very high-spirited and largely untrained and gave the novice owner a lot of trouble. First it was one thing, then another, but finally he was discovered one morning to have disappeared from his stable. Foul play was not suspected nor did the poet at this stage adopt the foolish expedient of locking the stable door. On the contrary he behaved very sensibly. He examined the stable to ascertain how the escape had been effected and then travelled all over the yard on his hands and knees looking for traces of the animal's hooves. He was like a dog looking for a trail, except that he found a trail where many a good dog would have found nothing. Immediately the poet was off cross-country following the trail. It happened that Chapman was on a solitary walking tour in the vicinity and he was agreeably surprised to encounter the poet in a remote mountainy place. Keats was walking quickly with his eyes on the ground and looked very preoccupied. He had evidently no intention of stopping to converse with Chapman. The latter, not understanding his friend's odd behaviour, halted and cried:

'What are you doing, old man?'

'Dogging a fled horse,' Keats said as he passed by.

Storm in a Teacup

Chapman had been reading a book on China. It contrasted the immense natural wealth of China with the poverty of her people. In this situation he described possibilities of making money, and excitedly discussed the matter with Keats.

'If we make a journey into the interior,' he explained, 'for once everything will be in our favour. The whole continent is littered with priceless antiques in gold, ivory, jade, silver, and porcelain. Since the people are wretchedly poor, they will sell them to us for practically nothing. Moreover, the cost of eating there is practically nil. It is the chance of a lifetime!'

At first Keats demurred somewhat. He knew that China was infested with bandits and, apart from that, he loathed rice. But he was won over to the proposition by the knowledge that Chapman would pay all expenses and that there seemed a genuine opportunity for making big money, which would naturally be shared fifty-fifty. Arrangements for the expedition were put in hand forthwith.

After exhaustive and futile attempts to make lucrative deals in the big cities and towns, they decided that their true interest lay in the ancient rural wildernesses where the most primitive poverty still existed. Accordingly, with modest mule train and retinue of coolies, they set out for the interior.

After long travel in strange and lonely places notably destitute of objets d'art, they came one morning upon an astounding spectacle. It was a public memorial probably four thousand years old – a gigantic teapot and set of teacups in the open air. The travellers, wildly excited, enquired who owned the monument. It was in the custody of a local but very impoverished mandarin. Sending for ladders, Keats climbed into the huge vessels with certain tools and geological instruments. After minute examination, he gave a frenzied roar at Chapman from inside one of the cups. All the vessels were made of absolutely priceless porcelain.

The pair interviewed the moneyless mandarin on the spot. He was most courteous but could not see his way to sell the monument to the honourable travellers for less than £100. With pretended reluctance, the travellers agreed. A deed of transfer was signed and a coolie despatched to the bank of the nearest town for the cash.

The following day Keats made an appalling discovery – something possibly well-known to the mandarin. Each of the cups alone weighed about two thousand tons, and the teapot weighed perhaps six thousand tons. To move the vessels would be quite impossible, no matter what gear or transport could be got. When Keats hastily told the mandarin that he could not go on with the transaction, the latter reproached him with such dishonourable and dishonest conduct. What excuse had he for such behaviour?

'I was in my cups when I made that offer,' Keats said.

Walden Pond

Many a time had Keats at the deep blue ocean gazed with brooding, covetous eye, occasionally aiding the latter with telescope. Across the turbulent waters, he often assured Chapman, lay the great new continent of America – land of fabulous opportunity, land of spices, El Dorado of every empty heart and wallet. Chapman would ask him why he did not seek his fortune in that land.

'I haven't the fare,' Keats would simply reply.

Chapman had certain enterprises of his own on hand; these involved consorting with rough sea captains and other iron, jersey-clad men who frequented the dangerous public houses of the water-front. Pondering the poet's problem, he took the advice of sundry blue-water friends and was soon in a position to tell Keats that the problem was solved: a passage to America had been arranged and it would not cost a penny. A pantry boy was required on a small passenger steamer. Demurring at first because the job was menial, Keats accepted.

This decision he regretted after the ship had left safe harbour, discovering that happy sailing is the exclusive lot of sailors; day after day he was continuously and monstrously sick. His employers were extremely angry as he was quite useless in the pantry and, in fact, could not be admitted to it. Moreover, everybody else on board, including some frail females, continued in perfect health. Indeed, one day the first mate contemptuously drew the poet's attention to this fact. 'O si sic omnes!' he managed to stammer.

After many trials, however, he penetrated to Boston where he chanced to meet an elderly though not unpretty lady, reputed to be of great wealth. Her obvious interest in literature made easy the poet's entrance to her gracious society. He laid careful siege, praised her expensive hats, and called her his Dark Lady of the Bonnets. She accepted his advances after a fashion, but made no attempt to settle a fortune on him, and would meet him only in the local park, by day.

Desperate, he decided to stake all on an offer of marriage. The lady's reply was peculiar.

'Have you ever read the works of our great writer Thoreau?' she asked.

'Never heard of him,' Keats said.

'Well, I happen to be his wife,' the lady said coldly.

'I do not think that need be an impediment to the realization of our divine love,' the poet said. 'Why not get a divorce a mensa et Thoreau?'

Not Cricket

Chapman once called upon Keats seeking advice on a delicate matter. It appears that he had accompanied his eldest son to a school cricket match. In the course of the day, Chapman found himself without cigarettes, and was told that the nearest shop was ten miles away. He took the obvious course of making his way to the visitors' cloakroom, which was then deserted, and carefully went through the pockets of the guests' overcoats.

His haul amounted to about seven packets and contentedly he went back to watch the play. A rather ironical thing happened the following day. The headmaster wrote to Chapman to say that Chapman's son was strongly suspected of having pilfered from guests' overcoats on the day of the match and that the question of expulsion was under consideration. What was Chapman to do? That was the question he posed Keats.

Keats advised that Chapman should reply saying that he had personally witnessed another boy going through the coats; that he did not care to reveal this boy's identity but that, in view of his own carelessness in not reporting the matter, he for his part would penalize himself to the extent of replacing all the missing property.

Chapman accepted this suggestion.

'I hope it will work,' he said. 'I believe there is a very bad atmosphere in the school since this happened.'

'It will clear the heir,' Keats said.

Beside the Brook

Chapman, by the same token, was somewhat of a botanist, and used to drag Keats out on hard cross-country walks in search of 'specimens' and whatnot. With them on each walk went a small hamper packed with sandwiches and whiskey. One day, when they were lunching quietly beside a babbling brook, Chapman accidentally spilled some whiskey on the sward. Being a provident and careful character, he patiently detached the little plant upon which the spirit had fallen, raised the leaves to his lips and drank down the golden drops. Keats enquired lazily what the plant was.

'Sorrel,' Chapman said.

'And that little bulb or heart in the centre,' Keats said, 'what is it called?'

'That,' Chapman said, 'is equivalent to the heart of a cabbage. Observe the delicate bleached leaf, notice how tiny and oval and hard the core is. Actually, where sorrel is concerned, the term used by us botanists is not "heart", but "egg". That is called the "egg" of the sorrel.'

'I see,' Keats said. 'Take care that it is not said of you that you would drink whiskey off a sorrel egg.'

Chapman took out his watch and began to wind it in the still evening.

Paris Fashions

Keats and Chapman once visited Paris in connection with a commercial idea which had originated with Chapman – that fashionable women could be induced to wear 'fur' coats made from the pelts of sheepdogs. They had spent a week in the French capital making attempts, all unsuccessful, to interview persons of standing in the fashion world. Chapman, who was wearing a sheepdog coat by way of sample, attracted much notice in his movement through the streets, not only from citizens but also from their dogs. The friends' financial resources had at length reached a dangerous level and they decided to return home on the morrow. After such a week Keats was not in the best of tempers but he glumly agreed when Chapman suggested a stroll along the quays in the summer evening preparatory to turning in for the night. They had not travelled far when they became aware of a commotion in the distance. They observed a man, who was shouting frantically, break away from a crowd which was apparently trying to restrain him, run towards the river and leap in. Immediately he began to drown and disappeared. Chapman, aghast at the sudden tragedy, cried:

'The man's gone off his head; he's mad!'

'He's in Seine,' Keats said.

Mexican Dog

One year, when Fortune had briefly beamed, Keats and Chapman took rooms for a spell in Dublin. A gas ring sufficed for the needs of their modest cuisine but they found it unsuited for heating the lofty Georgian apartments in deep winter. Keats made some enquiries and was later in a position to inform Chapman (whom he believed to be retaining a few hidden pounds) that if the latter could buy a certain type of stove, the gas company could supply a special fuel known as 'alco'.

Chapman, an amateur lexicographer, knew that this word was stated in the reference books to mean 'a small variety of dog found wild in Mexico and Peru, and now domesticated', but doubtfully accepted the poet's assurance that in Dublin it meant a coke-like combustible substance. And Chapman bought the stove, also giving Keats some money wherewith to buy a load of 'alco'. Keats, taking Chapman by the arm for a quiet walk, explained that the company had been constrained, through the vast volume of orders, to entrust some of the deliveries to certain private hauliers who, en route, with the load, had devised a secret method of extracting from it an intoxicating distillate. The result was, the poet added, that if the load arrived at all, it was spilled all over the street instead of into the coal-hole, and made off with by passing urchins. For that reason, he had deemed it inadvisable to invest Chapman's money in this fuel, but had instead acquired an interest in two African gold mines.

'Who on earth is this?' Chapman gasped, seeing a strange creature approaching in the street.

'He looks like one of the alco-haulics,' Keats said.

Triple Murder

Just after the first production of the famous Manitoba wheat strain, Keats read a book on the subject, became immensely interested and bought a farm to test the claims made for the seed. To make certain that the ploughing and sowing method used were impeccable, he imported from Canada three very elderly farmers and put them to work on his lands.

The farmers did some work at the beginning but were badly affected by the European climate and eventually took to drink. Their potations increased with time, their work diminished, and the first season's crops were a complete failure. Their reply to the row kicked up by Keats was a demand that he should forthwith keep his promise to pay their passage home any time they asked for it.

The poet, who was almost ruined by his disastrous experiment, lapsed into a mood of murderous resentment. Into his mind came a deadly resolve: he would pay no passage home nor would any of his three senile and fraudulent servants ever see home again. He decided to kill them. And straightaway he began to put doses of arsenic in their food. Of this he did not say a word to Chapman.

One morning Chapman was horrified to find the three old men stiff and dead on their rough pallets. He ran and acquainted Keats. The poet affected to take the news philosophically, remarking that the men were all over the allotted span; he then suggested that they should be buried on the farm.

Chapman was appalled at so cavalier a procedure and said that the simultaneous death of three men however old, followed by their immediate interment in farmlands, might give rise to suspicion. Keats pondered this and agreed, saying that the observation was very proper and that he would arrange for a post mortem before burial. It happened that he knew a very ancient and broken-down doctor who would do practically anything for a few shillings.

And so it was arranged. The doctor made a great incision

in the dead men's abdomens, glanced at certain organs, and certified that death was due to natural causes, i.e. old age. The bodies were duly buried by night.

But Chapman was worried by the perfunctory nature of the proceedings and, after some days' brooding, he suggested to Keats that it might be safer to have a second post mortem carried out by a famous specialist.

'I see no point in re-opening old sowers,' Keats said curtly.

Haute Cuisine

Keats and Chapman once went into a very expensive restaurant and ordered roes of tunny or some such delicacy. The manager explained apologetically that this dish had just gone out of season. Keats, however, insisted and the manager promised 'to see what he could do'. We do not know whether he called in the aid of some other restaurant, but the desired dishes were eventually produced. The two diners gorged themselves delightedly. Then Keats began to hum a tune.

'What's that you're humming?' Chapman asked.

'The last roes of summer,' Keats said pleasantly.

A National Note

Chapman, ever grimly aware of the unworldliness of the poet Keats, was continually preoccupied with schemes for making money. Having visited a circus, he told Keats he was convinced there was a fortune to be made in exhibiting wild animals and began discussing the possibilities of an expedition to India for the capture of sundry lions, elephants, and rhinoceri. Keats pointed out that these were very large animals which would be very costly to feed and which would require a vast hall for show purposes. Furthermore, it was possible to get killed pursuing them.

Chapman reluctantly agreed but suggested that the modest first-floor flat they occupied had possibilities as a show premises. The house had a spacious yard. If the back sitting room were filled with chairs and the yard with giraffes, it might be possible to get two shillings a head from persons anxious to inspect the necks and heads of those animals. Keats again objected: giraffes were very difficult to capture, and there would be insuperable transport difficulties; they would have to be transported by road and there were immense numbers of low bridges on all routes.

The two friends debated the problem far into the night. The poet's superior mental powers eventually posed a solution. Human curiosity, he explained, was provoked not only by what was enormous but also by what was tiny. Let them by all means establish a circus, he said, but let it be a flea circus! Chapman was delighted.

But one thing he insisted on. While ordinary trained fleas would do for the body of the act, there must be a star flea of exceptional size, strength, and ferocity.

Keats mentioned the conditions of war and rapine obtaining in Ireland. He suggested that in that land the correct type of flea could be found. Chapman agreed and, pressing the bulk of his slender savings into the poet's hand, bade him repair to Ireland, be as frugal as possible, but not to return flealess.

Keats departed. After some weeks he returned, looking remarkably fit and stout. Yes, he had the flea. For safety, he had it locked in the interior of his broken Hunter watch. The price? Fifty pounds.

Chapman was aghast. *Fifty pounds?*

'I don't care how strong and ferocious he is,' he expostulated, 'how can you justify paying fifty pounds for a flea?'

'He was in the Movement,' Keats said.

Warp and Woof

To change the subject. Have you any good yarns? Do you like yarns? Do you know what a yarn IS, apart from the fact that it is usually very long, and associated with a worm.

The silk-worm 'spins' a microscopically fine filament, and a yarn is the combination of hundreds of these strands, involving expensive machinery and human skill. If a homogenous textile could be found, of the consistency of fine twine, the whole clothing business would be in revolution, and probably coal would be delivered in sacks made from carpet material (in contrast with the present practice of making carpets from sacks).

A foreigner of undefined nationality once advertised a boast that he had invented this unitary unwoven thread, and invited offers from people interested in purchasing his rights in the invention. The notice caught the eagle eye of Keats, who in due course went along with Chapman to interview the inventor.

The latter showed the two friends many samples of the sensational new product, and then launched into a sales talk of unprecedented elaboration and enormity. Chapman was most impressed but Keats, continuing to finger and examine the thread, remained suspicious.

'How do I know that this isn't a yarn?' he asked.

Do It Yourself

Keats once complained bitterly to Chapman about a bore who had seized on him, brought him home, and discoursed for hours on the vast amount of money that could be made by an industrious person in his spare time. The bore showed the poet a great variety of articles which he had made himself – dry batteries, lamp-shades, wooden toys, dolls, button-hooking machines, coloured twines, and so on. He claimed to have sold great quantities of such articles to local shopkeepers. After some time, when Keats was too limp to make much protest at the whole dreadful performance, he explained that his most remunerative line was indoor games and that there was a fortune in homemade chessmen, draughts, ringboards, and dartboards. He then propounded a scheme whereby Keats and himself in partnership would produce a thousand dart sets, himself to make the boards and Keats to make the darts. He explained that darts could easily be made by hand without any tools.

'Without waiting for my agreement,' Keats said very sourly, 'he had the cheek to ask me where I would like to make the darts.'

'What was your reply to that?' Chapman asked.

Keats hesitated.

'I made a dart at the door,' he said, rather shamefacedly.

The Fire of Genius

Chapman came home very late one night to find Keats glumly working at an enormous manuscript. The poet said peevishly that he wanted a cup of tea, and to 'drum up' one quick. Chapman hastily put some water into a little metal pot they had, but found the fire was nearly out. He did his best to revive it with newspapers, old pieces of cardboard, and some sticks but the feeble little flames he produced obviously had little calorific content. After a time Keats looked up and sourly asked what was keeping the tea.

'This damn fire is nearly out,' Chapman said. Keats got up, surveyed it, then went back to his table, picked up the great wad of pages, and rammed them in under the pot. Chapman was aghast.

'My dear man,' he cried, 'your poems, your work...!'

The poet spat coarsely.

'Bah,' he said. 'It was only a pot-boiler.'

Witch-doctor's Brew

Once upon a time Keats and Chapman were on Safari in the Pacific and, by chance observing Easter Island, paddled their canoe towards it and landed. They marched inland, wondered at the great flocks of sheep which were grazing there, and happened upon the village of Hanga-roa on the west side, where the natives are confined with small allotments for tillage.

After laborious search Chapman found a native who understood a little English. This man told Keats and Chapman that he would introduce them to the resident witch-doctor, but warned them to be careful of him as he had immense magical powers and could even bring the great statues to life. This witch-doctor turned out to be a very old leper decked out with beads and paint. Chapman, ever sceptical, arranged for a litter to carry himself, Keats and the witch-doctor to one of the statues. In front of it the doctor lit a fire, produced a pot and in it made a stew of snakes, toads, rats, and sundry maggots. As the unholy smoke and smell rose from the cauldron, he began incantations and gestures, dancing about and uttering strange calls. To his utter horror Chapman saw the expression on the face of the great statue change: there seemed signs of breathing in the chest and the arms were twitching.

'It's alive!' Chapman screamed and collapsed in a dead faint. But Keats was not in the least intimidated. He smiled and advanced with an outstretched hand.

'Dr Living Stone, I presume?' he said pleasantly.

On an Urn

Keats and Chapman, consumed somewhat by a not too genuine enthusiasm for archaeology, spent some uneasy months in the stone townlands of Cyprus, Greece, Turkey, and Persia. Their desultory researches were not improved by the climate, their respective tempers suffered severely from mosquitoes, and for once Chapman was the first to betray a breakdown of manners.

One evening he was toying with a vile peppermint drink in the foyer of their shanty hotel when Keats stumbled in, a dirty vase protruding from his pocket.

'What have you got there?' Chapman asked morosely.

'A small thing but Minoan,' the poet retorted, recklessly firing it at his interlocutor.

From the Vasty Deep

Keats and Chapman were induced to attend a spiritualist meeting and it happened that the lady who was conducting negotiations with the other world was not only very pretty but smiled very nicely right throughout her trance. Towards the end of the session Chapman, who had conscientious objections to truck with spirits, suddenly leapt up and floored the lady with a right to the jaw. A bystander made the comment that this was very extreme behaviour.

'Not at all,' Keats said. 'On the contrary, my friend is a most moderate character. He likes to strike the happy medium.'

To Be Beside the Sea

Keats and Chapman were leading a precarious existence at Eastbourne. Going out one morning, Keats said:

'There's a character parked down here on the front, I want to get into conversation with him and into his good books. I will explain later but suffice it to say now that he is very old, very sick, and very wealthy.'

Chapman found all this to be true. The patient, cheerful, but very fragile, was wheeled down in a bath-chair every morning when the weather suited and left to take the sun for some hours on the promenade.

The two friends needed little more than courteous salutation to become amicably embroiled in his company. They drew up a seat to each side of the bath-chair and day by day the dazzling converse of Keats ranged over the entire fields of mechanics, philosophy, dietetics, poesy, hydraulics, sewage, farms, optics, war, and the menace of the grey squirrel.

This went on day by day to the old man's delight, though his affliction (whatever it was) was clearly getting worse. One morning he was missing and soon there was news that he had died. Keats told Chapman that it was pretty certain that they would be substantially remembered in the will.

Weeks passed and one evening Chapman, distraught, white-faced, burst into the digs.

'Do you know what that wretched old buffer has done?' he shouted. 'Left all his money to a cat's home!'

'Well, perhaps I might have known it,' Keats said glumly. 'I knew he had an aid-to-puss complex.'

Party of Poets

Keats once invited a crowd of rather scruffy poet persons to his rooms, to the great disgust of Chapman.

The latter fumed through several hours of conversation of great preciosity. Finally in a tantrum he pulled Keats aside.

'These fellows are bores,' he whispered fiercely, 'and furthermore, I am not going to be further imposed upon by the said bores. I am going to retire for the night.'

'They are better than bed sores,' Keats said.

The Powder of Life

Once Chapman, by alcohol goaded into the boudoirs of passion, fell in love with an English lady diver. She accepted his attentions with some reserve, having noticed on every visit he was under the influence of alcohol. A professional performer at galas, she was known as 'The Plunge' and was faithfully followed by Chapman through a lengthy provincial tour. Keats tried to discourage the affair, having ascertained that the lady was poorly paid and had but small savings. Chapman, however, was not to be dissuaded and grew daily in whiskey-drinking and infatuation. In due course the lady, having been badly bruised in an embrace by the numerous small whiskey bottles in Chapman's pockets, absolutely refused to see him further unless he stopped drinking and carrying bottles on his person. Keats, consulted by his distressed friend on this situation, devised a method of solidifying the rye whiskey to which Chapman was addicted, subsequently breaking down the intoxicating solids into a white odourless and tasteless powder. Chapman referred to this substance as his 'indigestion powder' and openly consumed it in the presence of his love, earnestly swearing that weeks had passed since 'drop of alcohol' had passed his lips. The lady, though puzzled by his ashen and quaking appearance, accepted his pleas of reform and the courtship continued apace. Eventually Chapman told Keats that he had made up his mind to ask the lady to marry him and, further, that he was determined to give up the 'booze'. Keats was alarmed at the latter proposition.

'So you're going to take "The Plunge"?' he said.

'I am,' Chapman muttered.

'Well, my advice to you is this,' Keats said. 'Put your trust in God and keep your powdered rye.'

A One-Man Keats

Chapman had once spent a foggy evening moping about the streets of central London and, feeling the atmosphere was doing no good to his chest, casually dropped into a theatre hoping, perhaps, to encounter a presentation of the *Oresteia* of Aeschylus.

He was astonished to see a man enacting a one-man portrait of...Keats! Worse, Keats was shown as a pietistical layabout, forever thumping his craw, imploring heaven for mercy and publicly saying his prayers at great length. Chapman grew more and more disgusted at this false picture and when the curtain fell hurried home to the digs to tell Keats. Strangely the poet seemed already to have wind of the outrage, and yet seemed calm.

'But good Lord, man,' Chapman said excitedly, 'he is showing you as an imbecile, a religious psychopath, and there is nobody else in question only you...'

'Yes,' Keats said evenly, 'I believe he is making a holy show of me.'

The Iron Horse

On one occasion Keats and Chapman, again finding themselves in straitened circumstances, approached a high transport executive and sought work as station masters in Class I stations. This unreasonable request was refused, but the impeccable credentials which the two friends presented induced the patron to offer them employment as railway policemen. Chapman was pleased but the poet's acceptance of the offer was surly and ungracious. These attitudes were maintained: on their joint patrols, Chapman was eager and unremitting in his enquiries and observations, Keats deliberately careless, anxious not to see the abuses he was paid to correct.

One day the pair were on duty in a signal box, charged with the behaviour of train crews. A long goods train approached, ignored the stop signal and steamed slowly past the cabin and disappeared up a line which had been closed to accommodate an incoming express. Chapman was aghast.

'Did you see them?' he cried. 'The driver, fireman, and guard were sitting on the floor of the engine playing cards!'

Keats shrugged elaborately.

'*Dulce est desipere in loco*,' he murmured.

The Road to Nowhere

Keats and Chapman were once in lodgings near a site where vast road construction works were in progress. One Sunday Chapman brought in to lunch a man whom he had met casually in the course of his morning walk. After lunch, this man indicated the great road-making machines and suggested to the two friends that the whole party should go down and start off the machines 'for a joke'. Chapman sternly denounced this suggestion, but the poet agreed that this harmless activity would fill out the afternoon. Chapman, piqued, stayed in reading a book while the two others went out to the machines. In due course rattling and clanking from without informed Chapman that the 'work' had begun. After some time Keats, looking somewhat disconcerted, reappeared alone and explained that his companion had been killed. He (the poet) had started the main machines, which were articulated, and had already laid several yards of concrete surface before he missed the other man. Investigations which he immediately made revealed that he had accidentally steamrolled his companion, who apparently had been examining the rollers unaware they were to start so suddenly; the steamrolled corpse was then dealt with by the other machines which followed the roller – pulverizers, granulators, cementlaying and grouting machines. Tiny bits of the man, Keats explained, could be discerned, bound into the road surface. Chapman was horrified. Crying that decency at least demanded that some attempt should be made to retrieve the body, he ran out to the road with a sharp-pointed jack-knife and knelt down, searching for and endeavouring to extract little fragments of mangled humanity. Keats looked on in silence.

The construction company's watchman, returning from a local tavern, was astounded to see a new length of road made and a strange man kneeling on it occupied with some strange task.

'What on earth's that man doing?' he asked Keats.

'Scraping up an acquaintance,' Keats said.

Watt's That?

Enough of that. Keats threw a little dinner party once to celebrate looking into Chapman's homework and invited the great electrician Watt. The poet put up a few decent bottles of Beaune and the meal proceeded merrily. Watt was somewhat of a joker and had several tricks that were done with the new-fangled electricity. He 'accidentally' dropped a piece of bread into his glass of wine. He muttered some exclamation of annoyance and then touched the glass with his ring. Immediately there was a blinding flash and a loud report and the bread was observed to hop out of the wine onto the table.

'Watt's bread in the Beaune will come out in the flash,' Keats said.

Turner and Lane

A number of disorderly readers have been sending me anecdotes on this theme. One concerns an unfortunate venture by Keats into the fine art business. Unprincipled people passed off all manner of fakes on him, including a large canvas signed 'J. M. W. Turner'. Chapman insisted that an expert opinion be obtained, and the poet reluctantly invited Sir Hugh Lane to inspect the work. Sir Hugh pronounced the work to be a gross forgery.

'The verdict at once threw the poet into a mood of gloom until Chapman, wishing to cheer him up, remarked, "Come, come – all is not gold that glitters." The poet retorted with a slight sneer: "But it's a wrong Lane that has no Turner."'

That reminds me of two things – first, my suggestion of some years ago that the Charlemont House side of Parnell Square should be renamed 'Hugh Lane'.

Secondly, my story about the time Keats began laying out vast sums on buying the copyright of various thriller and blood-and-thunder books, believing that he was the J. J. O'Leary of his day and that there was a fortune in pulp publications. Chapman was aghast, predicted that the poet would lose all his money. Keats was adamant that the idea was a gold mine.

'All that glisters is Nat Gould,' he said.

Here is one more:

Keats once met the distinguished German violinist Herr Krauschmerz and invited him to stay at his 'place' for a week. Herr Krauschmerz, who enjoyed the hospitality of large country houses, accepted, but suffered a severe shock when conducted to a back-street hovel and invited to a supper of ray and chips which Chapman had been sent out for. Worse was to come. The bed he was shown to contained not so much a mattress as a collection of hard lumps held together with coarse canvas. The violinist spent a night of agony and was up at dawn in a furious temper. Chapman, who heard the guest moving about, arose to ask whether he would like a cup of cocoa but was soon, very pale-faced, back to Keats to relate the state of the violinist's temper.

'He is going round the place,' he said, 'like a bear with a sore head.'

Keats was unperturbed.

'He is a Herr with a sore bed,' he said.

Enough!

The Brother

Adapted by Eamon Morrissey from the writings
of Myles naGopaleen and originally staged at
the Peacock Theatre, Dublin, in 1974.

Introduction
Benedict Kiely

Utrum Frater Sit?

Behind every genuine Dublinman there may be another man, invisible as a rule: the Brother. There are the Mazzy and Dazzy, of course, and the Aunt Maggie, but these venerable figures can frequently be seen with singing family parties in pubs on Sunday afternoons. The Brother is more elusive even if he is also omnipresent.

The question is: what is a genuine Dublinman? The authentic Dublin accent can still be studied in all its glory in the markets in Meath Street, in the Liberties on a hill south of the Liffey, or in the Moore Street markets north of the Liffey. Vast new suburbs are inhabited by people who were born in Dublin and who have thus some claim to citizenship – although a first generation born from rural parents is not quite above suspicion. It is not yet twenty years since a genuine Dublin Gaelic football team, unreinforced by teachers or civic guards from rural places, won for the first time the All-Ireland county football championship.

The best workable definition of the Dublinman was made by the late Séamus Kavanagh, the actor, who was himself so much Dublin that he used to joke, but with much justification, that O'Casey had him in mind, in pre-vision, when he wrote the part of Captain Boyle for *Juno and the Paycock*. Kavanagh would say: 'Just look at me, bullet-head and all.' Kavanagh was a man for definitions. Incest, for instance, was 'cashing a cheque in your own bank'. A Dublinman was 'a man who doesn't go home for his holidays'. In other words, he was at home and didn't have to pack the cardboard suitcase tied with string and head off into the wilderness beyond where the tram-tracks used to end. A Dublinman lived at home.

The curious thing about the Brother as Myles presents him through the medium of The Voice is that he doesn't: he lives in lodgings or digs. No place further from St Stephen's Green or O'Connell Bridge than Skerries or Arklow are much mentioned, and these are adjacent seaside resorts and within the Dublin sphere of influence. The language of the narrator is always Dublin, in idiom and intonation: Brian O'Nolan, although no Dublinman by birth, could often get these things even better than James Joyce could: he had spent more time than Joyce had in the Dublin pubs. Yet the Brother does not live at home. There's a mystery here that may have some connection with the use that Flann O'Brien makes of uncles and brothers in *The Hard Life* and *At Swim-Two-Birds*.

The Voice that tells of the superhuman capacities and deeds of the Brother belongs to a person who inhabits the same digs and is also a brother, but not the Brother. The Mazzy and Dazzy are never mentioned but there is an uncle (eccentric ?) in Skerries.

The narrations take place at bus stops, possibly the same bus stop, and the Superior Type of Citizen (Higher Civil Servant?) listens attentively but is always non-committal. Another voice intrudes once to hint darkly that the Voice that talks about the Brother may also belong to a criminal type, at least or at best, a con-man or a cheap toucher and also a fantasist: 'I would not be surprised to hear that he has no brother at all.'

This, though, is unthinkable. The Brother exists and the proofs are indubitable. He is a healer, not a conventional doctor, though: he wouldn't allow one of them fellows into the digs. He is simply a layman who understands first principles. He also keeps an eye on the Guards, the officers of law and order, to see that they do their duty, that they don't smoke in doorways when on patrol or drink on the quiet when they have a chance. He is well-known in high places, in Dublin Castle, in the offices of the higher officials of Dublin Corporation. He is a stickler for propriety – every joke made in the digs is 'right', if you know what I mean. He knows and reads a lot, is near to all-powerful, is wise in politics and economics, is an authority on the French nation and their avidity for art; and on the odd ways of sea-lions who come, as is well-known, out of the sea, their young with them, to sit at night in the tramcars in the garages – and upstairs!

He's an authority on quaternions and well-known as such in the Institute for Advanced Studies – then in Merrion Square. To crown it all: he can unbend like any normal human being. He enjoys a joke – although it always seems to be at the expense of somebody else, the landlady or the other lodgers. He did even once get incapably drunk, but then it was on Christmas Eve whiskey.

Not even brotherly love could invent such a paragon. The Voice is telling the truth. The Brother exists: somewhere out there along the route of the 52 bus which used to take off from the Scotch House on Burgh Quay. Here it comes. Cheers. And don't back horses, as the man said.

A good selection from the 'Cruiskeen Lawn' column of material relating to the Brother is to be found in the volume already mentioned, *The Best of Myles*, edited by one of his brothers, Kevin O'Nolan. What Eamon Morrissey, a most talented young Irish actor, has done in his one-man show, *The Brother*, is something rather different, condensing into two hours an interesting showcase of many aspects of Flann–Brien–Myles.

Eamon is the Voice and the Brother is much spoken of, but the show does not confine itself to the Brother alone. It takes a few liberties with the original text: the fundamentalist may perhaps object to the treatment in the script that follows of the episode from *At Swim-Two-Birds* about the little man who discussed Rousseau, and was puked over by Kelly, close to Lad Lane police station. But I feel that if the three-headed author had himself decided to put on a formal floor show this could have been it. Quite frequently he put on an informal floor show and very good he was at it.

The opening is as good, or as bad, as macabre: the horrors of drink, the shakes, the flying snot, a gruesomely comic death by explosion, a fearful philosophical acceptance of outrage and abomination. Then that decent man, Bottle O'Bass Quinn, has the misfortune to get the crack of a doorknob on the kneecap ('Did I tell you that it all took place in a public house?'), and right after that the Voice is into theatre criticism in relation to the Abbey Theatre: 'There wasn't a laugh anywhere in it [i.e. the play] bar the wanst when a fellow slipped going out a door. He nearly creased himself.'

When the reader comes to, 'You see the Brother says that we were both employed by your man as characters', the sudden switch may be confusing. The 'your man' there referred to is not the mad brother-in-law who blew up the house but Flann O'Brien, one of the trinity, and you are back in the world and with the techniques of *At Swim-Two-Birds*.

Williams and Woods, of course, are famous manufacturers of jam: and whatever the English, Scots or Welsh may think the 'far side' is always Britain. The war referred to is the Hitler war. Naas, Newbridge, and Leopardstown are sacred, or accursed, names to those who play the ponies.

When the Voice tricks up his costume and makes a platitudinous political speech he is the eponymous character from *Faustus Kelly*, a satire on Irish political life that Myles wrote for the Abbey Theatre.

Jack fleas as large as mice bark at prison warders when the Voice is, for a while, a member of the Gardái: and the script also contains that classic short horror story, or story of the horrors, the final turn of the screw on Charles Jackson's *The Lost Weekend* which, by comparison, is positively sentimental.

From all of which the script drifts into the section of *At Swim-Two-Birds* that enshrines the celebrated poem by Jem Casey, the workers' poet: 'A Pint of Plain is Your Only Man'. Plain or single – a Guinness porter is no longer available. And then into one of the pulp-wild-western fantasies from the same book.

There is an odd story from the times of the Troubles – the 1920 vintage not the Troubles now proceeding. Ireland has never had any shortage of troubles. It seems that the unseen and silent friend (Sean) on the far side of the wood and glass partition is a man who has the unusual distinction of being born for Ireland, not of dying for Ireland.

Then there is a voice from the condemned cell telling a story that makes Poe's 'The Telltale Heart' seem perfectly rational: and the actor's work ends with that meditation on life and death and on the number that also ends *At Swim-Two-Birds*.

BENEDICT KIELY

118

Part One

The setting is the snug, or cubicle secluded from the public bar, of a Dublin pub: an institution (i.e. the snug) now vanishing off the face of the earth. The entrance is to the centre. The snug is shielded by a wood and glass partition and contains a small table and chair. On one wall there is a hatch through which drink is served. On the other a rack on which some coats hang. There is a public telephone on the downstage end.

The man who enters is the owner of the Voice which, according to Myles, tells us all we know or all we need to know about the Brother. An average type of decent Dublinman but now obviously shattered with alcohol. (That could also be average.) He raps on the hatch and gestures for a pint of stout and a small whiskey, i.e. a pint and a small one. Hangs hat, overcoat on rack. Returns for drink. Eases himself into chair with great care. Everything is shaking, water spilling all over the place. Foosters in pockets for cigarettes, dropping matches all over the place. He lights, has spasm of coughing, drinks. Clattering of teeth on glass. More coughing. He fixes glassy stare on audience.

Bedam, but you know people talk a lot about the drink. Whiskey and all the rest of it. There's always a story, the whiskey was bad, the stomach was out of order and all the rest of it. Do you know what I'm going to tell you (*pauses impressively*)? Do you know what I'm going to tell you? Do you know what it is (*holds up cigarette*)? Do you see that? That thing there in my hand. Cigarettes them lads, they're the killers, they have me destroyed. (*Paroxysm of coughing.*) I wouldn't mind that stuff at all, the drink. I mean you know where you are there. There's eatin' and drinkin' on that. Damn the bit of harm that ever done anyone, bar taken to excess of course. But this, these lads have me destroyed. (*Pulls hankie from pocket, applies shakily to ear, and blows nose smartly all over himself.*)

You heard, of course, that I was in digs. Ah yes, in digs again after seventeen years of the happiest married life any man ever had. And I'll tell you what was a great consolation. The two of them was buried in the same grave. Ah, yes. The two is in the one grave. The two is in the one grave and I'm back above in Heytesbury Street in digs with the Brother. You heard about the mad brother-in-law coming home on a visit out of the British Army three-quarters in the jigs?

Ah yes, he came in one night with three bottles in him and a serviette out of the B & I dining room. I told Mary the wife to lave him alone.

'Give him his head,' says I, 'and he'll be all right.'

Well in any case he began to fooster around the house and inside the hour he has the stairs on fire. I ordered all hands to the pumps, so to speak. We got the fire out after about an hour, but in the meantime this character is inside in the kitchen with all the taps in the gas meter full on, full bore. In any case the wife goes in and offers him a cigarette to get him out of the place, and the next salute is the whole kitchen is blun up and the wife killed on the spot, without a scratch on your man. He then gets a hold of a sledge-hammer when I'm doing the needful about the wife and away up with him into an attic under the rafters. And I'll tell you one thing about this man, a decenter chiner never wore a hat. Bar he was jarred.

Well in any case, when I got the wife's body covered under blankets, the brother-in-law was working on the ceiling with the sledge-hammer, working from above, and didn't the unfortunate poor man knock a lump of plaster down on Nicky, the eldest boy. Killed him outright. After that our friend passes into some class of a coma. A hard case if you like. A character. I suppose I could call him my best friend. But a divil when he had the few jars on him. In any case I sent a message for the Guards and the doctors to come but at eight in the morning this character wakes up and says he's off for the day to go to Killarney on the Radio Express. How are you! There was I with the wife and the eldest dead, the half of the house in ruins——and I wouldn't mind only on the way out he kicked the milk bottles to pieces and the young chisler Tomaus roaring his head off for his breakfast.

That's the way I'm fixed at the moment. That's the way your man has me written anyhow. He's very unthinking your man when he does be above in the bed writing me and the Brother. He puts me to no end of trouble just for the sake of an oul word. There's an example there. 'I wouldn't mind only'. The trouble he put me to just to get that out of me in the latter and, 'I wouldn't mind only'.

Not that I mind being back in digs. The landlady is AOK and I have the Brother for company. But your man has gone so contrary with the writing that you wouldn't know where you'd be in the morning or who he'd have you as.

The Brother is taking a very poor view of it and is thinking of taking it further. The law. Not that the Brother would think of going to the solicitors. Foot, he says, he would not put inside one of them fellas' offices. Hooks he says they are with the office on a weekly tenancy and a season ticket to Belfast waiting to skip as soon as they lay their hands on some poor orphans' dough. The Brother wouldn't go near them and do you know something? The Brother knows more law than any ten of them fellas put together.

He didn't need the help of any of them fellas in 1934 when he made the landlord take down and rebuild the back wall and replace gutters and pull the joysces out in the front drawing room and put in new ones.

Oh your man may start to worry when the Brother gets his teeth into him about the law. You see the Brother says that we was both employed by your man as characters, and your man has only got the right to use us as such and that we can't be pushed around doing every Tom, Dick, and Harry that your man thinks up when he's perched above in the bed writing books. Oh leave it to the Brother he'll fix your man, that is of course if his health holds out. The Brother is a martyr to the bad health.

The Brother is having terrible trouble with the corns. Ah yes. Sure the corns has nearly finished him with the ball-dancin'. Not that he complains, of course. Word of complaint is a thing that never passed his lips. A great man for sufferin' in silence, the Brother. Do you know what I'm going to tell you? A greater MARTYR than the Brother never lived. Do you know that? Talk about PAINS. He's a great example to all of us.

Number one, the eyes isn't right. Can't see where he's

goin' or who is shoutin' at him half the time. Number two, he does have all classes of shakes in his hands of a mornin'. Number three, he does have a very bad class of a neuralgia down the left side of his jaw and a fierce backache in the back as well. And of course the bag does be out of order half the time.

But do you know a game he does be at? He does spend half the day eatin' pills. He does have feeds of pills above in the digs. And do you know why? Why? Because he bars the doctors. He'd die roarin' before he'd let them boys put a finger on him. And of course half the pills he does be swallowin' is poison. POISON, man. Anybody else takin' so many pills as the Brother would be gone to the wall years ago. But the Brother's health stands up to it. Because do you know he's a man with an iron constitution. He's a man that would take pills all his life and not be killed by them.

Of course then the bag is out of order. Going round like a poisoned pup. Gets the pain here look. A great man for taking care of the bag, the Brother. But where does it get him? I mean to say, I wouldn't mind a man that lifts the little finger. Whiskey puts a lining like leather on the bag, so a man from Balbriggin was telling me. But the Brother doesn't know what to blame. Hot water three times a day if you please and this is what he gets for his trouble. All classes of pains in the morning. Breakfast on top of the wardrobe in the bedroom and then (*sniff, sniff*) *what's that smell* months afterwards. There is nothing so bad as a bad bag.

Sits picking at blackheads on face or hand.

There's a thing I was going to ask you for a long time. Is there any cure for blackheads? Sulphur is good of course for the pimples but they take time of course. You can't get rid of pimples in one night. They say the man for blackheads is steam. They tell me if you steam the face, the pores you know will open. Use plenty of steam they say.

I'll tell you what it is of course. Bad blood is back of the whole thing. When the quality of the blood isn't first class out march our friends the blackheads. It's nature's warning. You can steam your face until your snot melts but damn the good it will do if the blood isn't right.

There'd be less consumption in this country if the people

paid more attention to their blood. Do you know what it is. The nation's blood is getting worse, any doctor will tell you that. The half of it is poison.

Blackheads are bad enough but a good big boil in the back of your neck that's the boy that will make you say your prayers. A boil is a fright.

I knew a man that never wore a collar for five years, five years, think of that. Oh a boil is your man. You walk down the street and here you are like a man with a broken neck, your snot hopping off your knees. Like that, look. Ah the boil is the boy that'll bend your back.

And I'll tell you what's a hard man too, a bad knee. They say a bad knee is worse than no knee at all. A bad knee and an early grave. Believe me that's no joke a split knee cap and where are you if you're gone on two knees.

I knew a man and it's not long since he died, a man be the name of Bottle of Bass Quinn. A right decent skin too. You never heard a bad word about Bottle of Bass Quinn. Well Bottle of Bass got a crack of a door knob in the knee. Now you might ask how would he get a crack of a door knob in the knee, and it's a question I can't answer. But when me poor Bottle of Bass got a blow in the crown of the cap, they tell me there was trickery going on, trickery of one kind or another. Did I tell you it all took place in a public house. Well when me hard Bottle of Bass got the crack he didn't let on to be hurt at all, not a word out of him. On the way home in the tram he complained of a pain, the same night he was given up for dead but Bottle of Bass had a kick in his foot still. A game buckoo if you like, bedamned but he wouldn't die.

'I'll live,' says he, 'I'll live if it kills me,' says he. 'I'll spite the lot of ye.'

And live he did. He lived for twenty years.

He lived for twenty years and he spent the twenty years on the flat of his back in bed. He was paralysed from the knee up. That's a quare one. That's a blow on the knee for you. A blow on the head would leave you twice as well off. A crack on the head and you were right.

Gets drink from hatch.

I seen that thing at the Abbey. Ah it's very well done and well acted but that was all. I mean you couldn't get a laugh out of it. I seen meself sitting there for two hours and I couldn't get a laugh out of it. You do like the bit of humour do you know. Ah it's heavy stuff about clergymen do you know. Very well done, but I couldn't get a laugh there anywhere.

I tell you what my dish is. Did you ever see *Double Trouble* be Laurel and Hardy. Them's a very mad pair, Laurel and Hardy. The fat lad is a terrible madman. Another time the pair of them was for bringing a piano up a long flight of stairs. Your man got stuck. Your man Hardy is above pullin' and sweatin' and the thin lad below was for pushin' the piano down and the other pushin' it up. Begob I nearly passed out with the laughin'. You'd hear the roars of me a mile off. I'd go anywhere for a laugh.

I remember long years ago a Saturday night never passed but I would be in the Abbey. There used to be a great laugh in them days. But I didn't fancy that thing I saw the other night. There wasn't a laugh anywhere in it, bar the wanst, where a fellow slipped going out a door. He nearly creased himself. I tell you what, there's a very queer class of a play going on there now. The sister Annie put on a show there for the Orphanage in the years gone by. Put on a great play she did, with step dancers and bagpipes, real Irish stuff. The Brother had bottles of stout for the band inside in the paybox. Great night it was. One of the bagpipe lads was found mouldy in Marlboro Street the next morning, kilts and all lyin' up against the railings.

Ah you could get a laugh in them days. But the thing the other night there was no laugh in it anywhere bar the wan. I seen meself yawn in the middle of it. I never seen a play it was so hard to get a laugh out of. There wasn't a laugh anywhere in it, bar the wanst, where a fellow slipped going out a door, he nearly creased himself, but that was all. But all the same when I seen it happening, you would have heard me roaring a mile off. Begob you would have heard me roaring a mile off...

The Brother was saying there that's one thing we have to be thankful for in any case. That your man was never greatly taken be the Abbey, and didn't much go in for the playwriting. Otherwise we would be stuck as God knows what in front of the public. And another thing the Brother says that if your man put us into plays, it's actors that would be doing us, and once you fall into the clutches of them buckos you may give up.

Luckily we was only stuck the wanst in a play he wrote, and that was bad enough. There was I chatting away as usual about the Brother, only to find meself hurtled into a goboy politician by the name of 'Faustus Kelly' scheming and conniving on me own about the things I'd say at the public meetings.

The 'your man' referred to above is, of course, Brien–Flann–Myles, and at this stage in the proceedings on the stage, Eamon Morrissey speaks as Faustus Kelly, TD, which is Irish for MP. Faustus is the eponymous character in a satirical play by Myles with the help of Flann and Brien.)
Kelly lights up.

Yes. Fair enough. I think I'll say a few words about the banks, and emigration that is bidding fair to drain our land of its life's blood and spelling ruin to the business of the community. The flight from the land is another thing that must be arrested at no far distant day. Please God when I get as far as the Dáil I will have a word in season to say on that subject to the powers that be. And of course the scandal of the Runny Drainage Scheme is another subject upon which I will make it my business to say a few well-chosen words. Other members may sing dumb if they choose. Other members may be gagged by the party whip. The opportunist and the time-server may not worry about such things.

I'm telling you now the country is in a very serious position. We must proceed with the utmost caution. Neither Right nor Left will save us, but the middle of the road. Rash monetary or economic experiments will only lead us deeper into the mire. What the country requires most is informed and strong leadership and a truce to political wrangling, jobbery and jockeying for position. We have had enough of that – too much of it.

And there is something more. If the people of this country see fit to send me to the Dáil, there will be scandal in high places. I happen to know a thing or two. This is not the time nor the place to mention certain matters. But this much I will say, that certain things are happening that should not happen. These things are known to me at least. I can quote chapter and verse. I have it all at my fingertips and in due time I will drag the whole unsavoury details into the inexorable light of day. No doubt they will seek to silence me with their gold. They will try to purchase my honour. Will they succeed? Will success crown their attempts to silence me? Will their gold once again carry the day and make me still another of their bought-and-paid-for minions? By God it won't, by God in heaven it won't. I will speak my mind freely and fearlessly. (*Changing*) Dear God I hope nobody heard me. (*Blackout.*)

The actor is once again as he was at the beginning of the performance.

That was bad enough for me but the Brother was worse off again. He was employed by your man at the time in the capacity of a tram conductor and was forced to speak in guttersnipe accent that occasioned him considerable mental anguish. That was bad enough but when your man had finished with him in the book, didn't he forget all about him and there was the Brother stuck as a tram conductor for six months, and him that was only issued originally with the summer outfit, and nearly got his death out of it when the winter come.

No wonder the Brother took such a poor view of your man. You see when me and the Brother went for interview with your man, he said he was looking for two characters for a book he was writing at the time.

'What kind of a book is it,' says the Brother.

'It's a salutary book on the evils of wrongdoing,' says he.

'Oh I see,' says the Brother.

Fair enough but the next thing was your man started going strange and didn't he put us into a cowboy book be the name of *The Prairie Rose* and me that was never on a horse in me life.

After that the Brother said he'd fix your man and got out the books again. Come home to the digs wan day with a big blue one under the arm. Up to the bedroom with it and didn't stir out all night. The Brother was above having a screw at the book for over five hours non-stop, and the door locked of course, there's a quare one. On the Sunday I seen the Brother below in the sitting room with the book in his hand and his nose stuck in it. So I thought I'd get on to him about it.

'What's the oul book about?' says I.

'The Law,' says he.

'Oh game and ball,' says I. 'Carry on.'

But of course the law and proceedings were quickly shoved aside when the alarm for grub was sounded and all hands were piped to the table. Anyway the Brother announced that we had a primy facie case, only to find that your man had taken our names off us and wouldn't give them back to us. And as the Brother says you'd be wasting your time going into court if you didn't have your name with you. The law he says is an extremely intricate phonenom. If you have no name you possess nothing and do not exist and even the trousers that are on me do not exist, although they seem to me as if they do. And how could you sign an official receipt or an important document if you have no name. The Brother says that will all have to be sorted out, and the first thing is to get the names back whatever they were. That set the Brother back a bit.

But the Brother is a great one for bouncing back. Matteradamn what happens he gets on top of it. The Brother had them all in stitches above in the digs the other night. Gob he was in right form. Sits down to his tea and has a go at the jam. Then he gives the old man a nudge and says he: 'Do you know,' says he, 'it's well for that crowd Williams and Woods.'

The old man, of course, only that the eyes do be movin' in his head you'd think he was a corpse. A desperate man for readin' books and all that class of thing. Takes no notice of the Brother at all. Then the teacher asks why. The landlady starts to laugh out of her, too well she knows the Brother. Then the lad from the bank asks why. Begob in two ticks they were all laughing and waiting for the word from the Brother. Of course, he goes on chawing and takes no notice.

After a while he looks up.

'WHY IS IT WELL FOR WILLIAMS AND WOODS? BECAUSE,' says he (and begob there wasn't a bit being touched or swallyed be this time), 'BECAUSE,' says he, 'they get money for jam!'

Well lookit. The roarin' and laughin' was something fierce. The old man begins to choke and the landlady laughs so much she takes her left hand away from her chest where she keeps it when she's drinkin' tea.

Course when it all settled down the Brother got serious and started in about the war.

The Brother was across on the far side last week. He says we have no idea. The Brother says you'll see the Americans in before the New Year and do you know what I'm going to tell you. The Swiss are thinking of having a go at the French, there's bad blood there you know, always was. Some of your men in Switzerland speak French, but don't run away with the idea that that makes them Frenchmen. The Brother takes a very dim view of the situation above in Africa, he says that kind of thing couldn't last – can't last. He says you'll see a Republic there before the New Year. He gives them till Christmas to blow up. Another crowd that aren't happy at all, so the Brother says, is the Swedes. A desperate crowd of men for going to sea. Close up the area with mines and torpedo boats and where are you? You're in for trouble. The Brother was saying that he has eighteen pounds of tea stored above in Finglas. He knew the war was coming five years ago. He said the thing couldn't last.

The Brother has it all worked out. The war. How we can get through the war here in the Free State. I mean the rationing and brown bread and all that class of thing. The Brother has a plan. Begob you'll be surprised when you hear it. A very high view was taken when it was explained in the digs the other night.

It's like this. I'll tell you. We all go to bed for a week every month. Every single man, woman and child in the country. Cripples, drunks, policemen, watchmen – everybody. Nobody is allowed to be up. No newspapers, buses, pictures, or any other class of amusement allowed at all. And no matter who you are you must be stuck inside in the bed there. Readin' a book, of course, if you like. But no getting up stakes.

D'ye see, when nobody is up you save clothes, shoes, rubber, petrol, coal, turf, timber and everything we're short of. And food, too, remember. It's work that makes you hungry. Work and walking around and swallying pints and chawin' the rag at the street corner. Stop in bed an' all you'll ask for is an odd slice of bread. Or a slice of fried bread to make your hair curly, says you. If nobody's up, there's no need for anybody to do any work because everybody in the world does be workin' for everybody else.

Telephone rings. He starts, then waits for somebody to answer it. Nobody does. He approaches it himself. Covers mouthpiece with hankie. Heavily disguised voice.

Hellow, who's speaking please. (*Normal voice.*) Is that Charlie? Well begob, I was thinking about you yesterday, what am I talking about, it was this morning with his nabs and the young wan with him down in Ushers Island. Zzzz zzzz. Indeed and I did. A Sahada day in Mrs Lawlors a Naas. *Zzzz zz.* Do you know what it is, that kind of thing can't last. I seen the same crowd in Newbridge on Easter Monday stuck inside in a back snug with four Free State Army privates, two supervisors, from the Turf Board, a certain lassie that you know and I know in the middle of them and the whole crowd singing Boulavouge.

I went out to Leopardstown the other day on the bike, lost a packet of course. Who do you think I seen?...Our friend... On the inside of course, getting the cards marked all over the place, with the big heifer of a wife in the fur coat.

Back in town about half past six, feel like a cup of tea and an egg; go into a certain place that you know and I know. Who do you think is there? Our friend. With the two dames sitting up there as large as life. Bowl of soup to start with, but not without the drop of madera in it. Know what he fancies next. A whole turkey between the three of them, working away there for hours chatting away, knocking back liquers thirteen to the dozen and a taxi tickin' away outside.

Now to my certain knowledge that man works in a certain department of a certain store and is paid three pounds fifteen a week, three pounds, fifteen shillings per week. What I want to know is how is it done...Leave that alone now. How is the missus Charlie? Is that a fact? Well do you know what it is, you are a terrible man...But sure it's only nature me dear man...You may bet your life on it...Hello, hello is that Charlie?

Replaces phone. Frightened and amazed. Then he recovers.

By the way, if you are stuck this is a good place to have a sandwich. They have a good clean woman to cut the bread and make the sandwiches. And cleanliness is all important. Lord save us there is nothing so disgusting as thumb marks on bread.

Stares at phone again.

That could be your man's doing. Maybe he's after waking up again. That's the only bit of peace me and the Brother get is when your man is asleep, which is most of the time. But as soon as he wakes and getting notions, he has the pair of us tormented. The sooner the Brother has a go at him the better.

Of course I could always get a name. Doyle maybe or Spaldman is a good name, and so is Sweeney and Hardiman and O'Gara. I can take my choice. I'm not tied down for life to one word like most people. I don't care much for Doyle.

Changes into policeman.

Mind you not everything your man had us doing was objectionable. Some of the things you couldn't help enjoying. There was wan in particular I thought I'd like. You see on wan of your man's few excursions out of the house didn't he get himself into trouble with the police, arrested and all he was. Anyway when it was all over, didn't he write about it and the next thing didn't I find myself as a policeman giving evidence against him. By God I was sure I was going to enjoy it, but it didn't turn out the way I wanted. (*Blackout.*)

Your Honour the defendant is charged with begging, disorderly conduct using bad language and with being in illegal possession of an armchair.

Last Thursday I found the defendant in the middle of a crowd in Capel Street. He was seated in an armchair and was cursing and using bad language. He was exhibiting a card bearing the words 'Spare a Copper, all must help each other in this cruel world'. He became abusive when I asked him to move on and threatened to take me on and any ten of my butties. He lay down in the gutter when I went to arrest him, and shouted at the crowd to rescue him saying he was a republican soldier. I had to send for assistance.

At the station the defendant stated that he was holding a political meeting in Capel Street. He was discussing monetary reform and mendicancy and had as much right to obstruct the thoroughfare as the Fianna Fail crowd.

Because of the unsanitary condition of the defendant, it was decided to remove him to Mountjoy, where he refused to take a bath in accordance with the lawful instructions of the prison governor. That will be the subject of a separate charge your Honour, but there are further charges in respect of offences committed while the accused was in custody. In Mountjoy, the defendant damaged the window of his cell, set fire to his bedding and attacked two warders, though not physically. No, not physically your Honour, he incited certain animals to attack the warders. Eh fleas your Worship. When ordered to take a bath the defendant became violent. In the presence of two warders he smashed the window of his cell. The warders were reluctant to pinion and overpower the prisoner for reasons that are now within the knowledge of the court. When warned by the warders, defendant dragged his bedding onto the floor and set fire to it. He then took off his old coat and threw it on the warders' side of the blaze. Immediately due to the heat the coat was subject to large-scale evacuations. Apparently some of the animals had wings or at least could transport themselves with considerable agility. The warders were attacked and badly bitten. One man is still in hospital. I myself was assailed and bitten by a flock of animals. Your Honour I seen Jack fleas as big as mice barking at me.

It was then decided to release the prisoner from Mountjoy, due to the danger to prisoners and staff alike, but he refused to quit the premises and had to be ejected with a hose, however he was found back in his cell the following morning. He had broken into the jail sometime during the night and had filed through certain bars which would cost the Offices of Public Works £9 18s. 5d. to replace. When found in his cell he was in an intoxicated condition using bad language and demanding cocoa.

It will be necessary to contact the Attorney-General with regard to further charges, but in the meantime your Honour, I would make a strong appeal for bail. I have been informed by the prison warders' association that if the defendant has no money they will be willing to throw in a few quid. As the head warder up there said to me this morning, your Honour, 'That man is infected with hoppers.' (*Blackout.*)

The actor is revealed sitting back at table with drink.

Did you see that picture *The Lost Weekend* about the eh... (*mimes drink*) all right of course, bits of it were good. Your man in the jigs inside in the bed, and the bat flying in to kill the mouse, that was damn good. I'll tell you another good bit, hiding the bottles in the jacks and there was no monkey business about that. I tried it since myself. It works but you have to use half pink bottles. Up the chimney is another place I thought of. And of course you can still tie the small bottles underneath the mattress. But what are you to do with the empties if you stop in bed drinking? There's a snag there. I often think they should have malt in lemonade syphons.

Don't talk to me about that lost weekend, sure haven't I been through far worse weekends myself, you know that as well as I do. Sure Lord save us I could tell you yarns. I'd be a rich man if I had a shilling for every morning I was down at the markets at seven o'clock in the slippers with the trousers pulled on over the pyjamas and the overcoat buttoned up to the neck in the middle of summer. Sure don't be talking man.

The last time I went up there was the time the wife went down to Cork last November. I won't forget that business in a hurry. That was a scatter and a half. I got the fright of me life. You won't believe this, but it's a true bill. The best you ever heard.

In the morning I brought the wife down to Kingsbridge in a taxi. I wasn't thinking of drink of course at all, hadn't touched a drop for four months, but when I paid the taxi off instead of going back in it, the wife gave me a look, nothing said of course. After the last row I was for keeping off the beer for a year. But somehow she put the thing into me head. That was about nine o'clock I suppose. I will give you three guesses where I found meself at ten past nine, in another taxi. Above in the markets and there wasn't a more surprised man than meself there. Of course in a way it's a good thing to start at it early in the morning because with no food and all the rest of it you are at home again and stuffed in bed before four o'clock. It's the late nights that are the killer, two and three in the morning getting poisoned in sheebins and all classes of hooky stuff and a taxi man on the touch. After nights like that it's a strong man that will be up in the markets in time next morning.

Anyway that was my first day back on it. The next day where was I, up at the markets before they opened, there was another chap there but I didn't look at him. I couldn't tell you what age he was or how bad he was. There was no four o'clock stuff that day. I was around the markets till twelve o'clock or so, then off downtown to get meself shaved by a barber. Then up to a certain hotel and straight into the bar. A whole crowd of them there that I know. What are you going to have and so on. No, no have a large one. So and so's getting married on Tuesday. Me other man's wife has had a baby. You know the stuff. Well Lord save us I had a terrible tank of malt in me that day. I had a feed in the middle of it because I remember scalding meself with hot coffee, and I never touch the coffee at all, only after a feed. Of course I don't remember what happened to me but I was back home the next morning with the clothes off.

By this time I was well into the malt. Out with me again feeling like death on wire, into the local, curing meself for hours. Spilling stuff all over the place with the shake in me hand, then back up to the hotel. I will give you a tip. Always drink in hotels. That way you can say you are meeting a party on business and are only having the one. It looks very bad to be seen in bars during the day time, it's a thing to watch that.

I met a few pals that day and the next thing I remember is waking up perished with the cold and as sick as I ever was in my life. Back up to the markets, taxis everywhere, and no food only a bowl of soup in the hotel.

How long this goes on I don't know. I'm all right in the middle of the day, but in the mornings I'm nearly too weak to walk and the shakes getting worse every day. By this time I'm getting frightened of meself. I say to meself, this will have to stop.

There's a pal of mine that's a doctor, this is in the hotel, who says he'll get me something to make me sleep, writes out a perscription and sends the porter out with it. Long shaped green ones the pills are.

'Take one,' says he.

But I know the doctor doesn't know how bad I am, so I took another in the jacks and two more on the bus home. I get into bed and I don't remember putting my head on the pillow. I wouldn't go out quicker if you hit me over the head with a crowbar.

Next thing I know I'm awake. It's dark. I sit up. There's matches there and I strike one. I look at the watch, the watch is stopped. I get up and look at the clock. Of course the clock is stopped, hasn't been wound for days. I don't know what time it is. I'm a bit upset about this. I turn on the wireless and try about a dozen stations and not one of them is telling what time it is. Then begob another thought strikes me. What day is it? How long have I been asleep with that dose.

What do I do but put on the clothes, and out to find out what time it is and what day it is. The funny thing is I'm not feeling so bad. Off with me down the street. There's lights showing in the houses. That means it's night-time and not early in the morning. Then I see a bus and then I see a clock. Twenty past nine. But I still don't know what day it is and it's too late to buy an evening paper. There's only one thing, into a pub and get a look at one. So I march into the nearest one quiet and correct and say 'a bottle of stout please'.

All the customers look very sober, talking very quiet you know. When your man brings me the bottle of stout, I say, I beg your pardon, but I had a few bob on a horse today and could he give me a look at an evening paper. The man looks at me and says what horse was it. It was like a blow in the face. I stuttered something about Hartigan's horses.

'None of his horses won today,' says your man, 'and there was a paper here earlier but it's gone.'

So I drink up the bottle and march out. It's funny finding out what day it is. You can't stop a man in the street and say would you have the right day please. God knows what would happen if you said that. I knew by now it was no use me telling lies about horses, so in with me into another pub, order a bottle and ask your man has he got an evening paper.

'The missus has it upstairs, says there's nothing in it anyway.'

I now begin to think the best thing to do is dial o, but I

think the girl might say hold on, and the next thing the box would be surrounded by Guards and ambulances and attendants with ropes.

Into another pub. I have the wind up now and no mistake. How long was I knocked out by the drugs, one day, two days? Was I in bed for a week? Suddenly I saw a sight to gladden my heart.

Away down at the end of the pub there was an oul fellow sitting at the counter reading the paper with a magnifying glass. I take a mouthful of stout and march down to him. Me mind is made up. If he doesn't hand over the paper, I'll kill him. I snatched the paper and read the date. Thursday 22 November. I never enjoyed a piece of news as much.

'Thanks very much for the loan of the paper,' I said, handing it back. I sat back in the seat a relieved man. Then it hit me. Today was Thursday fair enough, but what day had I gone to bed. Just how long had I been under that dose.

Well I nearly collapsed. Put me head in me hands, like that. Then I had it. And do you know why? Because there was no beard. I must have been to the barber's for a shave that morning, so I had only been in bed the wan day. It was the barbers that gave it to me. Do you see it pays to keep yourself neat.

He looks into the lounge bar by standing on a chair and looking over the partition.

No sign of him. Of course he wouldn't be in there with the hob-knobs.

Did you ever hear of the poet Casey. He was a poet of the people. A plain upstanding labouring man, the same as you or me. A black hat or a bloody ribbon, no begob not Jem Casey. A hard-working well-made block of a working man, with the handle of a pick in his hand like the rest of us. Now say there was a crowd of men with a ganger all working there laying a length of gas pipe on the road. Here at one end of the hole you have your men crowded up together in a lump smoking their butts and talking about the horses and one thing and another.

But take a look at the other end of the hole and here is me brave Casey digging away there on his own. None of your horses or your bloody blather for him. Here is me nabs saying nothing to nobody but working away at a pome in his head with a pick in the hand and the sweat pouring down off his face from the force of his work and his bloody exertions. That's a quare one. Not a word to nobody, not a look to left or right, but the brain box going there all the time. Just Jem Casey a poor ignorant labouring man, but not a poet in the whole world who could hold a candle to Jem Casey. He was a man who could meet them and beat them at their own game, now I'm telling you.

Now I know what I'm talking about, give a man his due. If a man's station is high or low he's all the same to the God I know. Take the bloody black hats off the whole bunch of them and where are you.

Give them a bloody pick, give them the shaft of a shovel into their hand and tell them to dig a hole and have the length of a page of poetry off by heart in their heads before the five o'clock whistle. What will you get? You'd be waiting around for bloody nothing. Yes I've seen his pomes and read them and...do you know what I'm going to tell you, I have loved them. Do you know what it is, I've met the others the whole bloody lot of them. I've met them all and know them all. I've seen them and I've read their pomes. I have seen whole books filled up with their stuff, books as thick as that table there and I'm telling you no lie. But begob in the heel of the hunt there was only one poet for me. And that man is Jem Casey.

I could give you out one of his pomes as quick as I'd say my prayers. Begob it's not for nothing I call myself a pal of Jem Casey's. The name or title of the pome I am about to recite is a pome by the name of the 'Workman's Friend'. Begob you can't beat it. I've heard it praised by the highest. It's a pome about a thing that's known to all of us. It's about a drink of porter:

> When things go wrong and will not come right,
> Though you do the best you can,
> When life looks black as the hour of night –
> A PINT OF PLAIN IS YOUR ONLY MAN.
>
> When money's tight and hard to get
> And your horse has also ran,
> When all you have is a heap of debt –
> A PINT OF PLAIN IS YOUR ONLY MAN.

When health is bad and your heart feels strange,
And your face is pale and wan,
When doctors say you need a change,
A PINT OF PLAIN IS YOUR ONLY MAN.

There are things in that pome that make for what you call
permanence.

When food is scarce and your larder bare
And no rashers grease your pan,
When hunger grows as your meals are rare –
A PINT OF PLAIN IS YOUR ONLY MAN.

What do you think of that now, its a pome that'll live, a pome
that will be heard and clapped when plenty more...ah but
wait till you hear the last verse man, the final polish-off:

In time of trouble and lousey strife,
You have still got a darlint plan
You still can turn to a brighter life –
A PINT OF PLAIN IS YOUR ONLY MAN.

There's one thing in that pome, permanence if you know
what I mean. That pome I mean to say is a pome that'll be
heard wherever the Irish race is wont to gather, it'll live as
long as there's a hard root of an Irishman left by the Almighty
on this planet, mark my words.

I first heard that pome the time I was working as a cow-
puncher in the Ringsend section of Dublin. Ah yes working
away down by the river in Ringsend and Shorty Andrews and
Slug Willard, the toughest pair of boyos you'd meet in a day's
walk. Rounding up steers do you know and branding and
breaking in colts in the corral with lasso on our saddle horns
and pistols at our hips. At night we would gather in the bunk-
house with our porter and all our orders, cigarettes and no
questions asked, school marms and saloon girls and after a
while bedamned but in would walk a musicianer or a fiddler
or a man with a fiddle or pipes and he would sit there and
play Ave Maria to bring the tears to your eyes.

One morning, Slug and Shorty and meself and a few of the
boys got the wire to saddle up and ride up to Drumcondra to
see me nabs Mr Tracy, the boss. Up we went on our horses
cantering up Mountjoy Square with the sun in our eyes and

the gun butts swinging at our holsters. When we got the length, go to God but wasn't it a false alarm.

'Get back to hell,' says Tracy, 'I never sent any message. Get back to hell to your prairies,' says he, 'ye pack of lousers that can be taken in by any fly-by-night with a fine story.'

I'm telling you we were small men when we took the trail again for home. When we got the length, bedammed but wasn't half our steers rustled across the border into Irishtown by Red Kiersay's band of thieving ruffians. Red Kiersay you understand was working for another man by the name of Henderson that was writing another book about cattle dealers and jobbing and shipping bullocks to Liverpool.

'Get yourselves fed,' says I to Shorty and Slug, 'we're going riding tonight.'

'Where?' says Slug.

'Right over to them their rustlers roost,' says I, 'before Mr Tracy finds out and skins us.'

So when the moon had raised her lamp o'er the prairie grasses, out flies the bunch of us, Slug, Shorty and myself on a buckboard making like hell for Irishtown with our ears back and the butts of our six-guns streaming out behind us in the wind. Shorty drew out and gave the horses an unmerciful skelp across the where-you-know, and away with us like the wind and us roaring and cursing out of us. I roared, bashing the buckboard across the prairie, passing out lorries and trams and sending poor so-and-so's on bicycles scuttling down side-lanes with nothing showing but the whites of their eyes. I smell cattle, says Slug, and sure enough there was the ranch of Red Kiersay ahead of us sitting on the moonlit prairie as peaceful as you please.

Down we got off the buckboard to our hands and knees and up with us towards the doss-house on our bellies, our eyes narrowed into slits.

'Don't make a sound,' says I, viva voce to the boys, 'or it's kiss me hand to taking these lousers by surprise.'

On we slightered with as much sound out of us as an eel in a barrel of tripes. Go to hell but a fellow pulls a gun on us from behind and tell us to get on our feet and no delay. Bedammed but wasn't it Red Kiersay himself, the so-and-so, standing there with an iron in each hand and a lucifer leer on his beery face.

'What are you at, you swine?' he asks in a real snotty voice.

'Don't come it Kiersay,' says I, 'we're here for our own and damn the bloody thing else. Come across with our steers or down I go straight to Lad Lane and get the police up.'

'Keep your hands up or I'll paste your guts on that tree,' says he, 'you swine.'

'You dirty dog,' says I between my teeth, 'you dirty swine you.'

Well the upshot was that he gave us three minutes to get out and out we got because Kiersay would think nothing of shooting the lights out of us and that's the God's truth.

'What will we do?' says Slug.

'Down to Lad Lane Police Station,' says I.

That's the very thing we done.

The station sergeant was with us from the start and gave us over to the superintendent. Nothing would do him but to give us a whole detachment of DMP to see fair play done and the fire brigade there for the asking.

'Do you know what it is,' says Slug, 'there's a crowd of Red Indians above in the Phoenix Park, wigwams and war paint and all, believe me. A couple of bob to the right man there and they are ours for the asking.'

'Right,' says I, 'go up and get them, and let the lot of us meet outside Kiersay's at a quarter to eight.'

After a while the policemen were rounded up and marched across the prairies to the Circle N, as fine a body of men as you'd hope to see, meself and the super at the head of them as proud as bedammed. When we got the length there was Slug and his Red Indians waiting for the word. In behind the buckboards with us to wait. Away went the Red Indians around the ranch-house, firing their flaming rods into the house. The whole place was flaming like billyo in no time and out comes Red with a shotgun and his men behind him, ready to make a last stand for king and country. Lord save us it was the right hard battle. Go to God if Red doesn't hold up a passing tram and take cover behind it, firing all the people out with a stream of dirty filthy language. I fired off me six bullets without stopping. A big sheet of plate glass crashed from the tram onto the roadway. There was a terrible scutter of curses and the boys began to get busy. We broke every pane of glass in that tram, raked the roadway with a death-dealing rain of six-gun shrapnel and took the tip off an enemy cowboy's ear. The policemen were firing off their shotguns, and waving their batons in the air. Shorty and myself, behind a sack of potatoes picking off snipers like bedammed. On went the scrap for half an hour and then bedammed but the enemy was weakening.

'Now is your chance,' says I to the super, 'lead your men over the top,' says I, 'and capture the enemy stronghold for once and for all.'

'Right you are,' says he.

Over the top with me brave bobbies, as bold as brass with their batons in their hands. The battle was over and here was me brave men handcuffed hand and foot and marched off down to Lad Lane Station. Good enough.

He looks at his watch.

Begob the landlady will have tea on the table. I'll see you later. (*Blackout.*)

Part Two

The actor comes onto the stage as in the beginning. Except that he walks with a stiff leg and there is the unmistakable sound of the squelching of liquid. He stops and speaks pleasantly to the audience.

Eh, the good lady, I trust she's keeping well. (*Hangs coat, more squelching.*) Oh I see what you mean. I know what you're at. But you needn't worry. I'm just wearing the Brother's patent trousers. The trousers are fitted with an eel-like pocket that reaches to the ground. The idea of the trousers do you see is to do away with the bother of the Saturday night brown paper parcel. You know the take-a-way stuff. The pocket is exactly the diameter of a bottle of stout. It is possible to stow four stouts in each pocket. Of course at first walking in the loaded position will be slow but you soon get used to it. But now you say what happens if you happen to get a belt in the leg or fall and the bottles get broken? And the answer is nothing. The pockets is stout-proof and the beer will lie safely in the bottom of the pocket, until it can be syphoned into a jug or directly into a guest's mouth in the privacy of the home. Indeed many people including the Brother prefer to drink the draught stout, and every night I bring home a pocketful for him. Straight past the landlady, no questions asked.

Of course there is a problem if you fill the pocket with draught stout. At all cost you must avoid crowded buses. (*He struggles to extract pocket.*) I mean if you're sitting there and a fat lady bangs herself down beside you, a great, cascade of stout will emerge from your pocket, ascend to the roof, rebound and drench everybody in its frothy brew.

He succeeds in getting the pocket out. It is three feet long. He hands it into the hatch. He says: 'The usual, Mrs.' He gets a drink and returns to his seat.

Who is going to win beyond? Which of the pair would you back? The Brother says your man is going to win. But begob I don't know. It'll be a long time before your other man hands in his gun. Your man is smart, I'll agree with the Brother there. And he doesn't take a jar, that's another thing that stands to him. And of course he bars the fags as well. But does that mean that your other man is a buff? Oh indeed begob it doesn't. It certainly does not. Because your other man gets up very early too. It wasn't yesterday or the day before your other man came up.

Of course the Brother looks at it the other way. He is all for your man and never had any time for your other man. Says no good could ever come out of the class of carry-on your other man has been at for the last ten years. There's a lot in that, of course. The Brother certainly put his finger on it there.

But it's not all on the wan side. Your man was up to some hooky work in his time too. There's a pair of crows in it. And I think your man is six to four on. Do you know why? Because he knows the place backwards, every lane and backyard in it. Lived there all his life, why wouldn't he? And of course your man doesn't know where the hell he is. And do you know why I wouldn't be sorry to see your man coming in first? Because it would be great gas to prove the Brother wrong for once.

He belches loudly

The Brother can't look at an egg. Can't stand the sight of an egg at all. Rashers, ham, fish, anything you like to mention – he'll eat them all and ask for more. But he can't go the egg. Thanks very much all the same but no eggs. The egg is barred. I do often hear him talking about the danger of eggs. You can get all classes of disease from eggs, so the Brother says.

The trouble is that the egg never dies. It is full of all classes of microbes and once the egg is down below in your bag, they do start moving around and eating things, delighted with themselves. No trouble to them to start some class of an ulcer on the sides of the bag. Just imagine all your men down there walking up and down your stomach and maybe breeding families, chawing and drinking and feeding away there, it's a wonder we're not all in our graves man, with all them hens in the country. I chance an odd one meself but one of these days I'll be a sorry man.

The Brother was on again about going for your man in the courts. Of course your man has done desperate things on the Brother. Any time he found the Brother enjoying the things he was doing, he'd do something woeful on him. Another time there he had the Brother doing a small dark man, a sort of expert on the subject of Rousseau, a member of the French nation. Well that of course suited the Brother down to the ground. Sure didn't the Brother raise the little finger with Rousseau. Many a time.

Anyhow, it was after the pubs closed and there was the Brother chatting away earnestly to a friend of your man's be the name of Kelly. Well of course I didn't understand the talk, but your man Kelly even though he'd had a feed of drink seemed to be taking it all in, standing near the Brother his head inclined in an attitude of close attention. Kelly then made a low class of a moan, opened his mouth and covered the Brother from shoulder to knee with a coating of unpleasant buff-coloured puke. All under the instructions of your man, of course. And the last that was heard of the Brother that night was of him shaking his divested coat and rubbing it along the wall. Maybe that's why in the digs, if the Brother is there, no one would dare mention the name of Rousseau.

There was always one thing that the Irish race was always noted for, one place where the world had to give us best. With all his faults and by God he has plenty, the Irishman can jump. By God he can jump. That's one thing the Irish race is honoured for no matter where it goes or where you find it, the jumping. The world looks up to us there.

There was a Sergeant Craddock in the early days of the Gaelic League who was sent along to a Gaelic League Sports Meeting and was challenged to jump be a man, a party be the name of Bagnall, the champion of all Ireland.

The two of them lined up and a hell of a crowd gathered to watch. Well Bagnall is the first off, sailing through the air like a bird and down in a shower of sand. What was the score? Twenty-two feet was the jump of Bagnall there and then. After the cheering died down Sergeant Craddock keeps his mouth shut, takes a little run and jumps twenty-four feet six inches – twenty-four six. There you are, go where you like in the wide world you will always find that the Irishman is looked up to for his jumping. The name of Ireland is honoured for it. Go to Russia, go to China, go to France, everywhere and all the time it's hats off and gra macree to the Jumping Irishman. Ask who you like they'll all tell you about it. The Jumping Irishman. It's a thing that will always stand to us, the jumping. (*He gives a tired little jump and examines it.*)

It's no wonder the Brother is dead set against your man. Get the names and we are away. Wan day the Brother brought me into the sitting room above, sat me down and locked the door.

'Now,' says he, 'have you any idea what the names are?'

'None at all,' says I.

'Would it be Mick Barry, the Quigleys, the Mulrooneys or the Hourimen, the Hardimen or the Merrimen. Scrutch, Lord Brad. The O'Browny or the O'Roortys?'

'Not them,' says I.

'Are we here at all?' says the Brother.

'That's another matter,' says I.

I mean if we are not the Brother and me, who are we? Maybe I'm one of the other fellows your man had me doing – like a barrister-at-law be the name of Mr Juteclaw. At the time I was council for a plaintiff be the name of Mr Smoke who was suing for grievous bodily harm and malicious damage to an attache case. The defendant was a well-known Dublin surgeon.

Lights change; he is attired as a barrister.

I appear for the plaintiff in this unsavoury case my Lord. And the action the defendant is taking against the well-known Dublin surgeon is in two parts. One: for causing grievous bodily harm, to wit the cutting off of a hand, and two: for causing malicious damage to an attache case. The history of the case, my Lord, is a sad one. My client is a decent working man, a trade unionist and a member of the Trinity College Fabian Society. In his childhood, my Lord, my client lost two fingers while learning Irish in a Christian Brothers school. The stubs of his missing fingers had never properly healed. My client as a consequence was compelled frequently to have recourse to medical men. In June of last year he visited the defendant, a well-known Dublin surgeon.

The object in visiting the defendant was to receive treatment for his complaint. He received no treatment whatsoever and was at no time given even what is commonly called the lamp. However after a period of inaction the defendant cut off the plaintiff's hand while he was under the effects of some strong drug or vapour, no doubt administered by the defendant. The plaintiff now found himself crippled for life and comes to court seeking substantial damages.

I realize, my Lord, that a hand must have five fingers, and not three fingers as the plaintiff had at the time of the offence. If a hand did not have five fingers the English language would be a mockery, a delusion and a snare. Since the plaintiff had only three fingers, perhaps your Lordship would note that the case 'cutting off a hand' was entered in italics.

In opening the second part of the case, my Lord, that of malicious damage to an attache case, I do so on behalf of my client since he is unable to do it himself since he is crippled.

May I display its interior to the court. As you can see the interior is extensively stained with blood, and I am instructed to say that this is the blood of the plaintiff. On the occasion of the bloody rendezvous that was to result in the loss of his hand, my client took the precaution of bringing with him in his attache case his pyjamas, understandably suspecting that he might wind up in hospital as a result of the treatment of the defendant. But when he emerged from his drugged stupor he was unceremoniously bundled into a taxi bag and all. When the plaintiff reached home, my Lord, he collapsed. Many months afterwards, when he had recovered somewhat, his landlady, a most respectable widow woman, asked him, when she was going on holiday, to give her a hand with the packing. He generously lent her his attache case. I will spare the feelings of the court as to what happened next, but I am bound to say that when the case was opened, it was found that he had indeed given her a hand with the packing, it having been placed there by this monster the defendant. (*He takes out hand and faints. Lights blackout.*)

At lights up he is Sergeant Pluck of The Third Policeman *walking with a bicycle.*

Did you ever hear of the mollycule theory? Everything do you see is composed of small particles of itself that are flying around in circles, arcs and figures too numerous to mention. Darting backwards and forwards all the time on the go. These gentlemen are called atoms, do you follow me?

Atomics are a very intricate theorem and can be worked out with algebra. Now when you hit a bar of iron with a good coal hammer, the atoms are bashed away by the wallops and some of the atoms of the bar will go into the hammer and vice versa. The gross and net result is that people who spend most of their natural lives riding iron bicycles over the rocky road-steads of this parish get their personalities mixed up with the personalities of their bicycles as a result of the interchanging of the atoms and you would be surprised at the number of people in these parts who are half people and half bicycle. Sometimes even worse. For instance I would reckon the post-man here to be seventy-one per cent bicycle. A round of thirty-eight miles on the bicycle every single day for forty years, hail rain or snow balls, there is very little hope of ever getting his number down below fifty again.

Now a man who is half a bicycle may not look like a bicycle, he would have no back wheel on him and you cannot expect him to grow handlebars. But a man that has let things go too far spends a lot of time leaning on walls or standing propped by one foot at kerbsides.

Of course there are other things to do with ladies and ladies' bicycles that I will mention to you separately at another time. And things I would rather not say too much about. For instance there was a young lady teacher in this district one time that had a new bicycle. She was not very long here when a man who was already half-way to being a bloody bicycle himself went into the lonely countryside on her female bicycle, bouncing over those rocky roads, but worse happened, when the young lady teacher rushed out to go somewhere in a hurry her bicycle was gone but here was your man's leaning there very conveniently and trying to look very small and comfortable and attractive. Need I tell you what the result was, or what happened. Your man had a day out with the lady's bicycle and her with the man's bicycle. And it's quite clear that the lady in the case had a high number, thirty-five or forty per cent I would say. Can you appreciate the immorality of that?

If a man's number is over fifty you can tell he has a lot of bicycle in him by his walk (*demonstrates*). He will walk smartly always and never sit down and if he walks too slowly or stops in the middle of the road he will suffer from the wobbles and fall in a heap and will have to be lifted and set in motion again by somebody. He will lean against the wall with his elbow and will stay that way all night in the kitchen instead of going to bed.

I will tell you a secret confidentially. My own grandfather was eighty-three when we buried him. For five years before his death he was a horse because he had spent so many years of his life in the saddle. Usually in his old age he was lazy and quiet but now and then he would go for a smart gallop clearing the fences in great style. Did you ever see a man on two legs galloping? His oul horse Dan, by the same token, was in a contrary way of thinking and gave so much trouble coming into the house at night, committing inditible offences and interfering with young girls during the day, that they had to shoot him. But if you ask me it was me grandfather they shot. And it is the horse that is buried above in Clooncoola Churchyard.

There were tragic cases too. I remember an old man. He was harmless enough but he had the people driven loopy by the queer way he moved and walked. He'd go up a little gentle hill at a speed of maybe half a mile an hour but at other times he'd run so fast you'd think he was doing 15 m.p.h. (*demonstrates*). Do you know what was wrong with the poor bugger, he was suffering from Sturmey Archer, the three-speed gear. *Stands up on chair again and looks into lounge bar. Then steps down and talks to audience.*

Still there Sean a Chara. Oh that's right ignore me. In the lounge with the big boys, a gang of ignorant pot-bellied sacrilegious, money-scooping robbers very likely runners from the bogs, hop-off-me-thumbs from God-forsaken places like Leitrim or the County Carlow. The sons of pig-dealers and tinkers. Like the Brother says them Government departments should be getting themselves more appropriate names. Surely, he says, the Department of Agriculture is a poor title, would it not be better to call it the Department of Yokel Government.

Walks with drink back to table

Which reminds me about the Brother. I've a quare bit of news for you. The Brother's nose is out of order. A fact. Some class of a leak somewhere. Well do you see it's like this. Listen till I tell you. Here's the way he's fixed. He starts suckin' the wind in be the mouth. That's OK, there's no damper there. But now he comes along and shuts the mouth (*demonstrating*). That leaves him the nose to work with or he's a dead man. Fair enough. He starts suckin' in through the nose. AND THEN DO YOU KNOW WHAT? THE WIND GOES ASTRAY SOMEWHERE. Wherever it goes it doesn't go down below. Do you understand me? There's some class of a leak above in the head somewhere. There's what they call a valve there. The Brother's valve is banjaxed. The air does leak up into the head, all up around the Brother's brains. How would you like that? Of course, his only man is not to use the nose at all and keep workin' on the mouth. O begob it's no joke to have the nose valve misfirin'. And I'll tell you a good one.

The Brother is a very strict man for not treatin' himself. He does have crowds of people up inside in the digs every night lookin' for all classes of cures off him, maternity cases and all the rest of it. But he wouldn't treat himself. Isn't that funny? HE WOULDN'T TREAT HIMSELF.

So he puts his hat on his head and takes a walk down to Charley's. Charley is a man like himself – not a doctor, of course, but a layman that understands first principles. Charley and the Brother do have consultations when one or other has a tough case do you understand me. Well anyway the Brother goes in and is stuck inside in Charley's place for two hours. And listen till I tell you. When the Brother leaves he has your man Charley in bed with strict orders not to make any attempt to leave it. Ordered to bed and told to stop there. The Brother said he wouldn't be responsible if Charley stayed on his feet. What do you think of that?

Of course Charley was always very delicate and a man that never minded himself. The Brother takes a very poor view of Charley's kidneys. Between yourself, meself and Jack Mum, Charley is a little bit given to the glawsheen. Charley's little finger is oftener in the air than anywhere else, shure wasn't he in the hands of the doctors for years man. They had him nearly destroyed when somebody put him onto the Brother. And the Brother'll make a job of him yet, do you know that? Ah yes, everybody knows that it's the Brother that's keepin' Charley alive. But begob the Brother'll have to look out for himself now with the nose valve out of gear and your man Charley on his hands into the bargin. Ah, well, of course, at the latter end he'll have to do a job on himself. HAVE TO, man, sure what else can he do? The landlady was telling me that he's thinkin' of openin' himself some night. You'll find he'll take the razor to the nose before you're much older. He's a man that would understand valves, you know. He wouldn't be long puttin' it right if he could get his hands at it. Begob there'll be blood in the bathroom anny night now. The Brother. O trust him to look after Number One. You'll find he'll live longer than you or me. Shure he opened Charley in 1934. He gave Charley's kidneys a thorough overhaul and that's a game none of your doctors would try their hand at. He had Charley in the bathroom for five hours. Nobody was let in, of course, but the water was goin' all the time and all classes of cut-throats been sharpened, you could hear your man workin' at the strap. O a great night's work.

Back to bar for more drinks. Orders. Stands up again on the chair briefly and looks over the partition.

I'll try again but ten to one he cuts me dead. Well Sean a Chara, how are we getting on at all? There you are I told you, I'll tell you about your man. I knew the mother well, the mother was a saint. (*Gets down off chair.*) As you know, I was Bart Conlon's right-hand man. We were through '20 and '21 together. Bart of course went the other way in '22. Anyway after a certain ambush in Harcourt Street there was six of us on the run. The six of us was marked men, of course. Orders come to us telling us that all hands was to proceed in military formation, singly by different routes, to the home of a great skin in the Cumann na mBan, a widow by the name of Darcy, that lived on the south side. We were all to lie low do you understand till there was fresh orders to come out and fight again. Sacred wars, they were very rough days them days. Will I ever forget Mrs Darcy. She was certainly a marvellous figure of a woman. I never seen a woman like her to bake bread.

Here was this unfortunate woman in a three-storey house of her own, with some quare fellow in the middle flat, herself on the ground floor and six bloodthirsty pultogues hiding above on the top floor, every man jack ready to shoot his way out if there was trouble. We got feeds there I never seen before or since, and the *Independant* every morning. *Outrage in Harcourt Street. The armed men then decamped and made good their escape.* I'm damn bloody sure we made good our escape.

We were there a week, smoking and playing cards, but when nine o'clock struck Mrs Darcy came up and Prodestant, Catholic or Jewman, and all hands had to go down on the knees. A very good...strict...woman, if you understand me, a true daughter of Ireland. About five o'clock one evening I heard a noise below and peeped out the window, sanctified and holy grandfathers.

What do you think but two lorries packed with military, with me nabs of an officer hopping out and running up the steps to hammer on the door, and all the Tommies sitting back with their guns at the ready. Trapped, that's a nice word trapped.

She was in the room herself with the teapot. She had a big silver satin blouse on her: I can see it yet. She turned on us and gave us all one look and said shut up yis nervous lousers. Then she foostered around a bit at the glass and walks out of the room with bang, bang to shake the house going on downstairs. And I seen a thing...she was a fine – now you'll understand me what I'm saying. I seen the fingers on the buttons of the blouse if you follow me and she leaving the room.

I listened at the stairs. This young pup is outside and asks in the la-di-daw voice, 'Is there any man in this house?'

She put on the guttiest voice I ever heard outside Moore Street and says, 'Certainly not at this hour of the night; I wish to God there was.'

The next thing I hear is madam this and madam that and sorry to disturb and I beg your pardon, I trust this and that. And then the whispering starts, and at the wind-up the hall door is closed and into the room off the hall with the pair of them. The young bucko out of the Borderers in a room with a headquarters captain of the Cumann na mBan.

After ten minutes we heard another noise. It was the noise of the lorries driving away. She saved our lives and when she came a while later she said, 'We'll go to bed a bit earlier tonight boys, kneel down all.'

That was Mrs Darcy, the saint.

Do you see what I'm getting at. For seven hundred years, thousands, no I'll make it millions, millions of Irishmen and women have died for Ireland. We never rared jibbers: they were glad to do it and will again. But that young man was born for Ireland. There was never anybody else like him. Why wouldn't he be proud.

A saint I called her. What am I talking about – she's a martyr and wears a martyr's crown today.

Makes telephone call.

Evenin'. I'm ringing you on behalf of your cousin, the Brother. Is her nabs there with you at the moment. Ah that's great because I'm ringing about the wedding. The wedding. The Brother wants to know about his present...his present. Of course the Brother wouldn't be the kind of fellow to give an ordinary class of a present. I mean none of your cake stands or china dogs for his nabs...He wants to make yis an offer...AN OFFER.

'Well I'll tell you what I'll do with him,' says the Brother, 'I'll make him the offer, give him the choice of the two things and he can talk it over with herself and they can make their minds up.'

'Number wan,' says the Brother, 'I'll pay for the wedding breakfast, hore derv, for all hands, cold chicken and ham, black pudding, custard and coffee, or,' says he, 'I'll foot the bill for eight clawhammers...clawhammers? Monkey-suits. In other words he's giving you the choice of a feed or a social wedding...Talk it over there yourself...Herself will take the clawhammers, but you'd prefer the feed...well I suppose you would feel a bit foolish sitting around drinking your stout in one of them things...O that's another thing. The Brother says that if yis are in the clawhammer there's to be no stout...No the Brother says that you'd get them all plastered with stains and that the clawhammer crowd would kick a barney when they got the suits back...That's that; there is to be no claw-hammers...oh herself is fighting...Hello hello, hold on a minute, stop fighting a minute, hold on, hold on all. The Brother foreseen all this.'

He did yes.

'If,' says he, 'there's any trouble we'll have to make a settlement. What I'll do,' says he, 'is to take the custard off the menu and hire only the wan monkey-suit.'

Well, for yourself, of course. Furthermore he will loan the best man his own blue suit. Now, and do you know what he'll get for the bride as well...orchards...Now are you happy, right, I'll tell him. (*Puts down phone.*)

All the same the custard will be a loss. (*Blackout.*)

Lights up: seated in a 'prison cell' – to be imagined.

The story I have to tell is a strange one, perhaps unbeliev-able, yet why should a man in a condemned cell lie. My name is Murphy, yet I have been found guilty of the murder of

Murphy and they say that my name is Kelly. Kelly and I were taxidermists.

Kelly ran the business and I was his assistant. He was the boss, a swinish overbearing mean boss, a bully, a sadist. He hated me but enjoyed his hatred too much to sack me. He threw me all the commonplace jobs that came in. If some old lady sent her favourite terrier to be done, that was given to me. Foxes and cats and shetland ponies and white rabbits – they were all strictly my job. I could do a perfect job on such animals in my sleep.

But if a crocodile came in, or a great borneo spider, or (as once happened) a giraffe – Kelly kept them all to himself.

Another thing was the smoking. For ten years in that little workshop he complained about my smoking.

'This place smells like a swamp, Murphy, your smoking those bloody cigarettes again.'

I impersonated Kelly well and enjoyed doing so behind his back.

Matters came to a head one day, when Kelly was in a filthier temper than usual. I had spent the morning finishing a cat and put it on the shelf with the completed orders. I saw him glaring at it.

'Where is the tail?'

'There is no tail,' I said, 'that is a Manx cat.'

'How do you know it's a Manx cat? How do you know it's not an ordinary cat that lost its tail in a motor accident. But you wouldn't know, because you are a slob.'

He called me a slob. On this occasion something within me snapped. The loathsome creature had his back to me, bending down to put on his bicycle clips. I picked up an instrument from the bench and hit him a blow with it on the back of the head. He gave a cry and slumped forward, I hit him again. I rained blow after blow on him. Kelly just lay there. I could find no pulse. There was no doubt Kelly was dead. I had killed him, I was a murderer.

As I stood there shaking, thinking and smoking, a mad idea came into my head. No doubt this sounds incredible, grotesque and even disgusting, but I decided that I would treat Kelly the same as any other dead creature that found its way to the workshop.

That evening I went to the workshop and made my preparations. I worked steadily all the next day. I will not appal you with gruesome details. I need only say that I applied the general technique and flaying pattern appropriate to apes. The job took me four days at the end of which I had a perfect face, skin and all. I made the usual castings before committing the remains of, so to speak, the remains, to the furnace. My plan was to have Kelly on view asleep on a chair for the benefit of anybody who might call. Reflection convinced me that this would be far too dangerous. I had to think again. A further idea began to form. It was so macabre that it shocked even myself. I would don his skin when the need arose, become Kelly, his clothes fitted me, so would his skin. Why not?

Another day's agonized work went on various alterations and adjustments, but by that night I was able to look into a glass and see Kelly looking back at me, perfect in every detail except for the teeth and eyes, which had to be my own.

Naturally I wore Kelly's clothes and had no trouble in imitating his unpleasant voice and mannerisms. On the second day, having dressed in the skin, I went for a walk, receiving salutes from newsboys who had known Kelly. Next day I was foolhardy enough to visit Kelly's lodgings. Where on earth had I been, Kelly's landlady wanted to know.

Why did that fool Murphy that works with me not tell you that I had to go to the country for a few days? No, and I told the good-for-nothing to convey the message.

I slept that night in Kelly's bed. I was a little worried about what the other landlady would think of my own absence. I decided not to remove Kelly's skin the first night I spent in his bed and as I lay there I eventually decided that Kelly should announce to various people that he was going to a very good job in Canada and that he had sold his business to his assistant Murphy. I would then burn the skin, own a business and would have committed the perfect crime.

Needless to say, I had overlooked something. The mummifying preparation with which I had dressed the inside of the skin was of course quite stable for the ordinary purposes of taxidermy. It had not occurred to me that a night in a warm bed would make it behave differently. The horrible truth dawned on me the next day when I reached the workshop and tried to take the skin off. It wouldn't come off, it had literally fused with my own. And in the days that followed, this process kept rapidly advancing. Kelly's skin got to live again, to breathe, to perspire.

Then followed more days of terrible tension. My own landlady called one day enquiring about Murphy. I said I had been on the point of calling on her to find out where I, he was. She was disturbed about my disappearance and thought she should inform the police. My Kelliness so to speak was permanent, it was horrible, but it was a choice of that, or the scaffold.

One afternoon two very casual strangers strolled into the workshop saying they would like a little chat with me. Cigarettes were produced. Yes indeed they were plain-clothes men, making a few routine enquiries. Murphy had been reported missing. Any idea where he was? None at all. No, he didn't seem upset or disturbed. Ah but, he was an impetuous type. I had recently reprimanded him for bad work. On similar other occasions he threatened to leave and seek work in England. Yes, I had been away for a few days myself, down in Cork. Yes, on business.

Then they put me under arrest for the wilful murder of Murphy, of myself. They proved the charge in due course with all sorts of painfully amassed evidence, including the remains of human bones in the furnace. I was sentenced to be hanged. Even if I could now prove that Murphy still lived by shedding the accursed skin, what help would that be? Where, they would ask, is Kelly? (*Fade-out.*)

Lights up.

I'll take that message now Mrs. Eh! (*Speaks through hatch.*)

The Brother was doing a bit of veterinary surgery. And an oul wan brought along her favourite cat that was sick. The Brother immediately diagnosed it as bladder trouble and it would have to come out. Which is what he did.

'A case,' says he, 'of letting the bag out of the cat.'

Ha, ha.

The long pocket arrives through hatch.

If I have no name at all, and my personality is invisible to

154

the law, then how could I be hanged for a murder I did not commit?

Am I completely doubtless that I am nameless? Positively certain. Would it be Mick Barry, Charleamange O'Keefe, Sir Justin Spens? Not that Kimberley, Bernard Fann, Bernard Poe or Nolan. One of the Gavins or the Moynihans, not them. Rosencranz O'Dowd? Would it be O'Benson? Not O'Benson.

My name is not Jenkins either. Roger McHugh? Not Roger, Sitric Hogan. Conroy. O'Conroy? Not O'Conroy. There are very few names that I could have then, because only a black man could have a name different to the ones I have recited.

Ah a poor class of a fellow that is only good for keeping nix while they steam open the new lodger's letters.

Is it life? I would rather be without it, for there is quare small utility in it. You cannot eat it or drink it or smoke it in your pipe, it does not keep the rain out and it is a poor armful in the dark if you strip it and take it to bed with you after a night's porter when you are shivering with the red passion. It is a great mistake and a thing better done without, like bed jars and foreign bacon. Many a man has spent a hundred years trying to get the dimensions of it and when he understands it at last and entertains the certain pattern of it in his head, be the hokey he takes to his bed and dies. He dies like a poisoned sheepdog. There is nothing so dangerous you can't smoke it, nobody will give you tuppence halfpenny for the half it, and it kills you in the wind-up. It is a quare contraption, very dangerous, a certain death-trap.
Polishes off last drink.

Maybe it has all started to effect me up here. Thirst is the man that will do that. Starts to effect you up here – in the attic. The brain gets dried up. The brain is like a wet sponge, do you know. There's a lot of moisture, blood and water and so on above in the brain – dry up that wet sponge and very queer things start to happen – very queer things. (*Lights fade slowly.*)

Numbers, however, will account for a great proportion of unbalanced and suffering humanity. Evil is even, truth is an odd number and death is a full stop. When a dog barks late at night and then retires again to bed, he punctuates and gives majesty to the serial enigma of the dark, laying it more evenly and heavily upon the fabric of the mind.

One man will rove the streets, seeking motor cars with numbers that are divisible by seven. Well-known, alas, is the case of the poor German who was very fond of three and who made each aspect of his life a thing of triads. He went home one evening and drank three cups of tea, had three lumps of sugar in each, cut his jugular with a razor three times and scrawled with a dying hand on a picture of his wife, goodbye, goodbye, goodbye.

As the actor takes the final curtain a human hand attached to an arm comes out of the hatch and salutes.